This is a work of fiction. Any resemblance to actual persons, living or dead, events, or locales is entirely coincidental.

Cover design by Isabel Robalo
Formatting by Caitlin Greer

ISBN 978-0-9966056-4-9

D1255615

1

Angel Bondesan watched her brother, David, in the living room of her apartment. She felt a rush of affection for him, his light brown hair falling into his face, narrow shoulders working while he stuffed clothes into his duffel bag.

They'd spent the last few months going through their father's things, talking about all the clues they had ignored that might have led to the truth about him. Angel had sobbed on David's shoulder when she missed Nico so much she felt like a gutted animal, and he'd been just as patient about listening to her rail out loud when she could muster her rage against Nico.

David had his own unfinished business with their father. Would he have eventually accepted David's sexual orientation? Did he love his son at the end?

People will tell you who they are if you listen.

It was something their father used to say, but now he was dead, and none of their questions about him would ever be answered.

David had insisted on spending spring break with her, and they'd passed the time taking long walks by the river that wound through town, talking and laughing, getting stoned, watching movies, and eating ice cream.

"Are you sure you have to go?" she asked.

"Classes start up again tomorrow." He turned to look at her, his forehead creased with worry. "But if you need me here, you know I'll stay, Ange."

The nickname caused a lump of sadness to rise in her throat, and she had to fight the urge to beg him to stay. He was her little brother. It wasn't his job to take care of her.

She smiled. "No way. I'll just miss you, that's all."

"Come stay with me anytime," he said. "Brad's a douche, but he won't mind, mostly because he'll spend the whole weekend hitting on you."

She wrinkled her nose. "Ew."

It was more than the fact that David's college roommate was an idiot. After the weeks she spent with Nico before Thanksgiving, every guy she met seemed like an ineffectual little boy. It didn't matter if they were thirty or if they were college guys like Brad, she felt nothing but a kind of benevolent pity for them. She'd only dated one man since she'd come home, a thirty-year-old music producer working on an album in one of the Hudson Valley's many small studios. But there hadn't been even a flicker of the heat she'd felt with Nico. She tried to tell herself that was a good thing. What she'd had with Nico was unhealthy, dangerous. It had killed her father, and it had almost destroyed her.

It was an unconvincing argument, even to herself. It was hard to settle for an unlit match when you'd had a wildfire.

"Well, the offer stands," David said, zipping up his duffel.

"Thanks."

He checked his phone. "You ready? The bus will be here soon."

She nodded, crossing the room and grabbing her keys. "Let's go."

They left the apartment and made their way down the narrow flight of stairs. The air was still wet from winter, slowly warming under the weak April sun. The streets were already teeming with students returning from break, and Angel felt an unkind hatred for them as she and David nudged their way around the crowds converging on the narrow sidewalks. She'd chosen to stay here before Nico's men had kidnapped her, but now it felt like purgatory. She was no longer the naive girl who believed her father was simply a wealthy real estate developer. Now she knew the truth; Carlo Rossi had been head of the Boston division of the Syndicate, a worldwide network of organized crime.

And he'd killed Nico's parents in cold blood.

It was hard to come back to the place where she'd once been so innocent. Hard to face her own denial and the loss of the person she'd once been. But the truth is, she didn't have anywhere else to go. She and David had inherited all of their father's property, including the apartments in Boston and New York City, but those places were too close to her father's work — and her father's work was too close to Nico Vitale.

Nico...

She pushed him out of her mind and turned her attention to the crowd gathering outside the bus station. "I hope you can get a seat," she said.

"I'll be fine," David said.

"You have your ticket?" she asked.

He pulled it from his bag. "Got it, Mom."

She smiled. "Very funny."

He looked at her for a long moment. "You sure you're okay, Ange?"

She nodded. "Yep."

He tipped his head. "Liar."

She leaned in to hug him so he wouldn't see the tears in her eyes. She was fine as long as nobody called her on her bullshit, as long as she didn't have to think about whether she was fine. But whenever someone got too close, she recoiled. Talking about her feelings meant talking about Nico, and that was like probing an open wound. Better to leave it alone. Maybe it wouldn't get better that way, but it wouldn't get worse either.

David squeezed her hard. She breathed in the scent of him; security and comfort and the aftershave he'd worn since he was sixteen.

He pulled back to look at her. "Promise you'll call if you need me."

"I promise. You?"

He nodded. "I promise."

"And don't let that asshole, Jacob, fuck with your head," she said. "You deserve better."

David had only come out a few months before their father's death, and he was still figuring out how to navigate the dating landscape at college. It had been a relief to listen to his guy problems instead of rehashing her own.

Not that she had any problems in that department. She and Nico were done. Because there was no way you could love the man who killed your father, even if your father had been a bad guy. Even if he'd been a criminal who had held a gun to your head.

She and Nico were done because that's the only thing they could be.

She and David turned as a bus pulled into the parking lot spewing black smoke.

"That looks good for the environment," David said.

Angel laughed in spite of herself. "When you're a famous writer, you can buy yourself a Prius."

"Deal." The bus pulled to a stop at the curb, and a few people got off before the crowd started climbing the stairs to board. He looked down at her. "I guess this it."

She forced herself to smile. "I guess so."

He wrapped her up in another hug. "I love you. Everything's going to be okay, I promise."

She didn't know if it was true. Didn't know if it could be true. But it was nice to have someone say it.

"I know," she said, giving him a final squeeze before she stepped back. "Now go on. Get a window seat."

He nodded. "See you in a few weeks."

"Margaritas and tacos," she said.

"Don't forget cabana boys," he added.

She grinned. "Can't wait."

They'd wanted to take a trip together over the summer, and while David had suggested Europe, Angel couldn't imagine going back to Italy or England without Nico. They could have gone somewhere else — Europe was big enough — but Mexico seemed like a safer bet. There she wouldn't have to remember Nico kissing her in the shadow of the Colosseum, wouldn't have to remember their final night together in London.

"I'll text you when I get in," David said, stepping on the bus.

She nodded, waving to hide the lump in her throat. She was being dumb. She'd lived alone for years before Nico had her kidnapped. But she and David had spent the last few months cleaning up their father's affairs, and she hadn't had much time to be alone with her thoughts. The magnitude of the trust left to them, the investments and charitable contributions and property, was overwhelming.

Then there were the businesses — both legal and illegal — to untangle. Angel had left most of that to Frank Morra, her father's Consigliere, but she knew that Raneiro Donati was putting pressure on him to get a permanent power structure in place.

And you did not mess with Raneiro Donati.

The problem was that there had been no Underboss in place at the time of her father's death. He'd been arrogant right up until the end, sure he'd be around to run his empire for a long time to come. Angela and David still didn't know what to do about it. How did you dissolve an illegal enterprise as big as the one run by Carlo Rossi without implicating everyone involved —from the soldiers who did his killing to the secretaries who had no idea they were covering for one of the country's most notorious mob bosses?

She and David had managed to issue an edict against several heinous income streams — human trafficking, high-interest loans to those who couldn't afford to repay them, the bullying of store owners to pay for protection — but Angel had no doubt there was plenty left to clean up. They would have to figure it out — and soon — but for now she presumed the remaining illegal business interests were still running under the auspices of the legitimate real estate company owned by her father before his death.

Owned by her and David now.

How would they untangle the illegal business interests from the legitimate ones?

She watched the bus pull away and waved until she lost sight of David's face. Then she started walking back into town for her shift at the record store. It was as good a place as any to distract herself from the mess that was her life.

2

Nico shuffled on the balls of his feet, moving quickly around the sparring ring at the center of the renovated gym. He was alone, the room dark around the spotlight inside the ropes, and he moved into a series of sweeps and knee jabs designed to disarm an enemy.

It had gotten harder to find sparring partners in the months since he'd started practicing Eskrima, a form of martial art that was so deadly it had been outlawed when the Spanish invaded the Philippines. He should have stopped sparring with his men long before he sent one of his soldiers to the hospital with a concussion. He had seen the looks on their faces when they worked together, knew his obsession was becoming dangerous. Then he'd gotten caught up in the moment, transported back to the dingy living room in London when Carlo Rossi had put the gun to Angel's head. A red wash of rage had blanketed his mind, and the next thing he knew, he was staring down at Paul, unconscious on the floor of the ring after a wicked elbow jab Nico had landed to the back of his head.

Nico had been horrified. Holding his own with the men was one thing; making them victims of his obsession was another.

Now he practiced only with his coach or when he was alone, reliving the scene with Angel's father over and over again, imagining an outcome in which he'd managed to disarm Carlo, even seriously injure him, rather than putting a bullet through his brain. Maybe then Angel would have forgiven him. Maybe they would even be together now.

"Boss?"

The voice caught him off guard, and he spun on his feet, ready to fight as he faced the door. He dropped his arms when he saw who was standing there.

"Luca." He hadn't been aware that he was breathing hard, but he was aware of it now as he spoke. "Is everything okay?"

Luca nodded. "Just here for the briefing."

"Is it that time already?" Nico asked. How long had he been in the gym?

"Ten past eight," Luca said.

Nico ducked under the ropes and grabbed his towel off one of the hooks. He wiped his face, then draped it over his bare shoulders as he crossed the floor of the gym.

"Is Vincent here?"

Luca nodded.

"Let me clean up," Nico said. "I'll meet you both in my office in ten minutes."

Luca held the door as Nico moved past, and Nico wondered if he was imagining the concern in his Underboss's eyes. It didn't matter. He wouldn't give credence to Luca's worry by addressing it. He was fine. Well, maybe not fine. He missed Angel. Missed her so fucking much that he felt like a sinkhole had opened up inside of him. Everything that mattered had been sucked into it, and he was still standing on the edge, peering downward, thinking maybe he should just jump in and get it over with.

He shook his head. That was weakness talking. His business — and his men— needed him, now more than ever.

He hustled up the stairs to his office suite and turned the shower on cold. Stripping off his shorts and tank top, he stepped under the spray, forcing himself to stand there until he was shivering. It was the only thing he seemed to feel, and he waited until his skin turned numb to climb out and towel off.

He walked into the adjoining bedroom and slipped on a clean pair of trousers and a short sleeve T-shirt. He avoided his apartment now, preferring the smaller, more intimate suite of rooms at his headquarters in Brooklyn. Here he could almost fool himself into thinking he was something other than alone, could almost feel part of the business he'd rebuilt in the wake of his parent's execution style murder at the hands of Angel's father.

Angel…

He had a flash of her, standing on the beach with her golden hair blowing around her face, her eyes as green and fathomless as the sea stretching out in in front of them. The memory hit him like a punch to the gut, and he was torn between wanting to hold onto it and wanting to banish it forever.

He chose the latter — or tried to anyway. It's not like she had given him a choice, and while he'd be lying if he said he didn't hope she would change her mind, banking on it would be foolish.

And he'd done enough foolish things because of his feelings for Angel Rossi.

He finished getting dressed and pulled a revolver from the top drawer of his desk. He still preferred to avoid the use of weapons, but he couldn't afford to stand on principle in such uncertain times. He was getting ready to close the drawer when his gaze settled on the rosary inside the drawer.

There had been a time when the meditative nature of the beads had soothed him, when his visits to empty churches all over the city had allowed him to feel closer to his parents. Now those things only made him bitter. What was the point in comfort if it only allowed you to pretend everything would be okay when it was all going to shit anyway?

He closed the drawer with a slam and made his way downstairs to the second floor conference room. Headquarters was quiet this time of night, with only the rhythmic hum of the machines in the cyber lab and the soft murmurs of the few people who stayed overnight to keep an eye on things. There were others in and around the building — more so in light of recent events — but they were all out of sight.

"Luca, Vincent," Nico said, sweeping into the conference room.

"Hi, boss," Vincent said.

He was a large man, and Nico had been embarrassed when he realized Vincent's blank face hid a keen intellect. Nico prided himself on seeing below the surface of things, and it bothered him that he had unfairly judged one of his soldiers. He'd rectified the situation immediately, moving Vincent into Luca's position when he made Luca his Underboss. That had been a forgone conclusion. Luca had stuck with him through the fiasco with Angel, had watched Nico's back when everything went to hell in the London flat.

But Vincent had been a surprise. He'd taken a bullet wound to the head — just a graze, but still — during the altercation with Carlo's men when they tried to rescue Angel. Since then he'd proven himself an asset in the management of sensitive issues that forced Nico to walk the moral line that was part of his next generation mob family.

Nico took a seat at the head of the table, Luca on his right and Vincent on his left.

"Tell me," he said.

Luca cut a glance at Vincent before returning his eyes to Nico. "Three more hijacked shipments, four men missing, possible breach of one of the databases."

"Four of our own?" Nico asked.

"And six more from other East Coast families," Luca said. He hesitated. "One of them from the Rossi family."

Nico tried to hide his alarm. He'd assumed the attacks on the Vitale family were isolated, aimed at him in the wake of Carlo's death. But that would mean they were perpetrated by someone in the Rossi family. That theory went out the window if they were losing people, too. He wondered if Angel knew. Word was Frank Morra was running things, and somehow Nico didn't see Frank keeping Angel and her brother apprised of the situation. Then again, Angel probably wanted nothing to do with it all anyway.

"Any sign of Dante?" he asked, revisiting an early theory.

"Not since the sighting in Brazil," Luca said.

Nico drummed his fingers on the conference table. His mother would have said Dante was like a bad penny, turning up everywhere. But the London police had placed guards by the door of Dante's hospital room, and Nico had been sure he would be sent away for a long time. He'd been enraged when Dante escaped, and he'd spent the next month milking every source he had for information. He'd even assigned someone to keep an eye on Angel, just in case the bastard tried to fuck with her. Nothing had happened, and a few weeks later, they'd gotten word that Dante was in Brazil. They hadn't heard a word about him since, and Nico forced himself to open his mind to other possibilities.

"What do you make of it?" he asked Vincent.

"It can only be one of two things," Vincent said. "Either the men are being taken as some kind of message, or…"

"Or?" Nico prompted.

"They're leaving voluntarily."

It was possible. Not everyone had been a fan of his twenty-first century vision of the business. Maybe the turf war with Carlo had pushed them over the edge. Carmine, his Consigliere and most trusted advisor, had warned him there might be dissent in the ranks. Raneiro, too.

Raneiro Donati. What would he make of this? As Nico's mentor and head of the Syndicate, the international organization that ruled over every organized crime family on the planet, Raneiro would have to know what was going on. But Nico had avoided asking him for help, knowing his patience had run thin in the wake of what happened in London. Nico hesitated to involve him again in business that should have been well under Nico's control.

And it would be. Nico would do whatever was necessary to see it done.

"Have you talked to the families of the missing men?" Nico asked Vincent.

"Claim to have no knowledge of their whereabouts."

"All of them?" Nico asked.

"All of them," Vincent said.

"Do you believe them?"

"I do."

Nico filed that away for later consideration and turned to Luca. "Tell me about the data breach."

"Sara Falco says there are signs that someone was trying to break through one of the firewalls."

"Trying?"

Luca shrugged. "She said it didn't look like anyone had gotten in, but I thought I should mention it."

"Because you think it's all connected," Nico said.

Luca sighed. "I think it's possible."

"How good is Sara?" Nico asked.

"Very good," Luca said. "She was in the Bureau's cyber training unit when we got her."

Nico shuffled the pieces inside his head. "I'll meet with Frank tomorrow. See if I can get a read on what's going on inside the Rossi family. In the meantime, I want a detailed report from Sara on the possible implications of the data breach and all the ways we can get in front of it."

"What about the hijacked shipments?" Vincent asked. "The men are worried."

"I pay them to transcend emotions like worry." He heard the steel in his voice and took a deep breath. He demanded total loyalty, total strength in his men, but alienating them wouldn't accomplish anything. "Tell them it's under control. No violence unless their lives depend on it."

"We're losing money - " Luca started.

"I don't care about the money," Nico cut him off. "Let's try to keep things from escalating until we can figure this out."

Luca nodded.

"Is there anything else?" Nico asked.

He suddenly wanted nothing more than to retire to his bedroom upstairs. To close his eyes and let the dreams of Angel come. It was the only time of day he could think about her without feeling weak. No man was in control of his dreams.

Luca shook his head and was rising to stand when a shrill ring sounded from his pocket. He removed his phone, looked at the display, and scowled.

"What is it, Morelli?"

Luca's face turned two shades paler, and a pit of dread opened up in Nico's stomach. His first thought was Angel. Could something have happened to her?

"What? Where?" Luca cut his gaze to Nico while he listened to whoever was on the other end of the phone. "Thanks for letting us know," he finally said. And then, "No, he's right here. I'll tell him."

He disconnected the call and turned to Nico. "It's Carmine. He's dead."

3

"Why don't you just call him?" Lauren asked the question from across the record store where she was alphabetizing a new shipment.

"What would be the point? Nothing's changed," Angel said.

She sprayed the glass door at the front of the store with window cleaner, then used long strokes to wipe it off. She'd quit her job at the Muddy Cup as soon as she'd gotten back from her father's funeral. She would never be able to work there again, never be able to lock up at night without thinking about the moment she'd been kidnapped by Nico's men. It didn't matter that Luca, one of her abductors, had become a friend during her captivity, or that she'd fallen in love with Nico. Dante was still out there, and even though Luca told her he'd been spotted in Brazil, the knowledge that he was free bothered her like an itch she couldn't scratch. She didn't want to relieve the moment it had all began, and she was grateful when Lauren put in a word for her at the record store.

"Perspectives change," Lauren said, dropping the last record into place. "Sometimes things look different after some time has passed."

"He killed my father," Angel said softly.

"But he did it to protect you, right?"

Angel could feel her friend's eyes on her back. Lauren was right, but it wasn't that simple. Angel had told Nico not to fire, had told him to leave, that she would be okay. Now it was impossible to know if he'd pulled the trigger to protect her or if some part of him — maybe a big part — had done it to avenge the murder of his parents.

It's not like she would blame him. Even outside the context of the law, unsanctioned killings of Syndicate family members were forbidden. Her father had killed Nico's parents to gain a foothold in the New York City territory. He'd done it for greed, plain and simple. She could understand why Nico felt the need for vengeance.

"It's more complicated than that," Angel said, crossing to the register. She avoided Lauren's eyes as she put the window cleaner under the counter.

"Maybe," Lauren said. "I just hate to see you like this."

Angel tried to laugh. "Like what?"

Lauren shrugged, her curly brown hair bouncing around her shoulders. "Sad. Sadder than usual."

"What's that supposed to mean?" Angel asked.

"You've always been sad, Angie," Lauren said. "But this feels different."

"My dad was murdered," Angel said.

Lauren knew that much; that Angel had been kidnapped and held for ransom. That she'd fallen in love with the man who had held her captive. But Angel had been spare with the rest of the details, telling Lauren that things had gone bad at the end and Nico had saved her life but accidentally shot her father. She hadn't told Lauren the rest; that her father had been a notorious mob boss. That compared to him, Nico looked almost like an upstanding citizen. Her father may have given her and David a different last name to protect himself, but in the end it had saved them from being associated with the Rossi crime empire. It was the only saving grace in a long line of shitty things that had happened since Nico's men grabbed her last October. The fact that the showdown with her father's men had happened in London helped; US news outlets weren't interested in much if it didn't happen within their country's borders.

"Have you thought about counseling?" Lauren asked, joining her behind the counter.

"I'm not ready to talk about it like that," Angel said. The words came out with more vehemence than she intended, and Lauren held up her hands in a gesture of surrender.

"Just a suggestion."

Angel sighed. "I know, and I appreciate that you care. I just need some more time to figure things out."

Lauren grinned. "Maybe some Thai food will help." She dug around in her bag. "I'll go pick up lunch."

"Let me give you money," Angel said, reaching for her bag.

"I got this one," Lauren said. "You can catch me next time."

Angel smiled. "Thanks."

"No worries." She headed for the door. "Back in fifteen minutes."

The bell on the door jingled as she stepped outside, and Angel was left alone in the quiet of the empty store. The majority of their customers were college students looking to kill time, but every now and then a collector would come in to buy one of the more valuable LPs. George, the owner of the store, must have made his money that way, because the store was nearly always empty.

She put Brand New on the turntable that was hooked up to the speakers, then started sweeping the old linoleum floor. She'd learned the hard way that silence was the enemy. That was when thoughts of Nico came creeping back, when she would see his panther eyes darken with desire as he tucked a piece of hair behind her ear, feel his breath on her lips in the moment before he lowered his mouth to hers. Then everything would come back to her — the safety she'd felt in his arms even when it didn't make sense, the completion she felt when he drove into her, making her his in a way no man ever had, in a way she feared no man would again.

She sang along to the record, slowly letting go of her thoughts. She'd protested the first time Lauren showed up at her apartment, determined to take Angel to her weekly meditation class. But it had been surprisingly helpful, and before long Angel actually looked forward to the sessions. It was the only time silence was tolerable, and willing her mind blank had become a kind of contest to see how long she could go without thinking of Nico.

The bell on the door rang, and Angel was surprised to see that Lauren had already returned.

"That was fast," Angel said. But she knew right away something was wrong. Lauren's eyes were wide, her chest rising and falling like she'd been running. "What's up?"

Lauren set her bag on the counter, then met Angel's eyes. "That guy… the one who kidnapped you…"

"Nico?"

Lauren nodded. "Nico Vitale, right?"

Fear unspooled in Angel's stomach, and she fought against the tide of panic. Had something happened to him? "What's going on?"

"I was waiting for the food," Lauren said. "They had the TV on the news. They showed his picture…"

Angel forced her voice steady. "What are you saying?"

"Someone close to him was killed. They're talking about the mob, Angel. Using words like execution." Her face was a mask of shock and worry. "Is that true? Is he part of the mafia?"

"What else did they say?" Angel asked, already rushing to grab her bag.

"Angel… this is not - "

"Just tell me what they said, Lauren," Angel snapped. "Please."

Lauren took a deep breath. "They said he's in hiding."

Angel headed for the door. "I have to go."

4

Angel paced the floor of her apartment while the phone rang in her ear. Luca had given her his number when he'd called to tell her about Dante. She hadn't thought she would use it. She liked Luca, had come to trust him, but she'd thought her association with Nico and everyone in the Vitale family was over.

She cursed when his voice mail picked up. "Luca, it's Angel. I just saw the news… What's going on? Is…" She lowered her voice, like someone might hear her ask about the man who killed her father. Like someone might know she cared so much that her heart was in her throat at the thought of something happening to him. "Is Nico okay? Please… just… call me and let me know, okay?"

She hung up and walked to the window overlooking the street below. Kids from the nearby college mingled with older people — many of them former students and teachers who had never left. It suddenly seemed so small, so removed from everything that really mattered. What was she doing here? How long was she going to hide?

She jumped as the phone rang in her hand. "Luca?"

"Angel," he said. "Hi."

"What's going on? I just saw the news." She'd opened her computer as soon as she'd gotten home from the record store, devouring everything she could find on the breaking story of Carmine Alfiero's execution.

"It's complicated," Luca said. "Is something wrong there? Are you okay?"

His questions threw her. "Me? I'm fine. Tell me what's going on."

He hesitated. "Nico wouldn't want you involved."

"That's not his call." She softened her voice. " Is he okay? I need to know, Luca."

He sighed, and she could almost see the worry in his blue eyes, the way he set his mouth into a thin line when he was trying to figure out what to do. "I don't know. He's not here."

"Well… where is he?" she asked.

"I don't know. Things have been… unstable."

"What does that mean?"

She heard his voice, muffled as he talked to someone else in the room, before he came back on the line. "It's a long story, Angel. Someone's after us, after Nico. We're not sure what's going on, but he's in hiding until we figure out what to do next."

"In hiding…" She took a deep breath. "Thanks, Luca."

"Angel, what are you - "

She hung up before he could say anything else, then pulled her overnight bag out of the closet. It took her less than ten minutes to pack and ten more to hit the highway.

She pulled onto the I84 and veered toward the water just north of Boston. The sun cast a blanket of diamonds over the Atlantic, bluer and brighter than it had been in November. She rolled down her window and let the briny smell of the sea wash over her as Nico's face filled her mind. She could never be near the ocean without thinking of him now, and she let the memories come, tears rolling down her face as she drove.

She'd stopped expecting it to make sense a long time ago. She loved him. It wasn't a product of her captivity or some kind of twisted delusion about who he was inside. She *knew* him. Knew him like she knew herself. She knew his tenderness and his kindness. Had seen his ferocious protectiveness over those he loved, his determination to do the most right thing in a business that was about as far from right as it could get.

She knew the other stuff, too. Knew he was a criminal. That he'd hurt and killed people, her father included, and that the work he did was in large part illegal. All of it should have been enough to stop the way she felt about him, especially with the distance between them after her father's death. But while it had been impossible to stay with him, to look at him in the wake of the loss, she'd never once convinced herself she didn't love him.

And there was something else; a question Luca had asked her the last time she'd seen him. They'd been outside the hospital before Dante's escape. Unable to face Nico, she'd been on her way to the airport to get on a plane back to the US.

"He did it to protect you, Angel," Luca had said. "You know that."

She had looked away, not wanting to see the plea in Luca's eyes. "He went too far."

"Really?" Luca had asked. "How far would you go to protect the ones you love?"

The question was still ringing in her ears months later. She wanted to believe she would walk the line more carefully than Nico, that if push came to shove, she would find a way around bloodshed. But the truth is, she didn't know the answer.

Now she could almost feel Nico out there, pulling her in like he had since the first moment he'd captured her with his amber eyes.

She pulled off the main road and headed for Bass Harbor, a tiny town set in a sheltered cove dotted with boats. She parked in a tiny lot overlooking the harbor, grabbed her bag out of the back seat, and headed away from the busy waterfront.

She continued along the water, heading toward the small beach houses and cottages that belonged to the people who lived there full time. She almost held her breath waiting for the dock to come into sight. Would it still be there? Had she imagined it all?

But no. A few minutes later, she saw the small platform that jutted out into the water. The boat wasn't there, and she sat down on the dock, letting her legs dangle over the water, hoping she wouldn't have to wait until morning. It was dusk, the sun setting over land somewhere beyond her shoulders. She could have called Nico. He'd told her as much when she'd seen him after her father's funeral.

If you need anything — anything at all — I'll be there.

She hadn't really thought she'd need him, not the way he meant. But still she'd kept his number, his name in her phone a tether to something she wasn't quite ready to let go.

The temperature dropped as the sun sunk lower in the sky, and she rubbed her arms, hoping she wouldn't have to wait until morning. A half hour later, she was about ready to walk into town and look for a cheap hotel when the sound of a boat motor got her attention. She followed the sound out over the water with her eyes, not daring to hope it was the right boat until it came into view. Or more accurately, until it's driver came into view.

She stood up and walked to the end of the dock as the boat coasted to a stop. The driver climbed out of the boat.

"Can't take you," he said as he tied the ropes to the steel cleats on the dock.

"You have to," she said. "I can't find my way back without you."

"Can't," he said, still not looking at her. "Don't work for you."

She swallowed hard, trying to think of the best way to make her case. "He... he needs my help."

It wasn't a gripping argument, but she thought it might just be the truth.

Ed looked up at her, his face creased with too many early mornings, too much salt and wind. He stood, staring at her silently for a long minute before speaking.

"I imagine you might be right about that."

"So you'll take me?" she asked.

He nodded. "Might mean my job, but I'd rather lose it than leave him out there like he is." He looked up at the sky. "Better get in, though. It'll be dark soon."

5

Nico watched the sky darken from the deck. It was soothing watching the water change from deep green to gray, then black as the light disappeared from the sky, and he let his mind drift to the two days he'd spent on the island with Angel. The waves crashing against the rocks, the rain battering the windows while he made love to her. While he made her his, exploring every curve and crevice of the body that had been made for him.

It was an exquisite kind of torture, but he must have been a masochist, because he didn't want it to end. Didn't want to let her go, even in his memory. Some days she seemed so close he could hear her say his name, breathless, the way she did right before she came. Other times he woke from the depths of sleep with her voice in his ear.

I love you, Nico.

The way she'd said it during the hours when they had been in a universe of their own making, the world dark and sleeping.

But as unbearable as the memories sometimes were, the other times were worse; the times when she seemed so far away he had to remind himself that she was in New York, just a couple of hours from the city. Then it seemed like she had been a figment of his imagination, a fever dream he would spend the rest of his life trying to recapture.

He noticed with surprise that night had fallen, and the beach had disappeared below the deck. He could hear the waves rushing toward the house, but he could no longer see them. He finally went inside to pour himself another drink.

He left the massive glass doors open, the sheer curtains billowing in the almost-summer breeze rolling in off the water. He couldn't afford to think about Angel now. He had bigger problems.

He poured some vodka into his glass and walked back outside, leaning on the railing of the deck. He still couldn't believe Carmine was dead. The older man had been an honorary uncle since Nico's birth, had been a fixture at every birthday party, every graduation. He'd helped Nico through the murder of his parents, had urged Nico to plan his moves carefully when Nico had wanted to indiscriminately unleash his fury. Nico hadn't always taken the older man's advice, but knowing it was there had been a comfort. And while Luca was as loyal as they came, it was Carmine who had the years of experience with the Syndicate — most of them working under Nico's father. In a business that bred suspicion, Carmine was one of very few people Nico trusted with his life.

And he'd been gunned down like a dog, just like Nico's parents.

Nico didn't understand it. His business had obviously been under attack for the past few months, but the disturbances had been minor — hijacked shipments, missing soldiers, suspicious activity on the servers that were locked down tighter than Fort Knox, guarded by hackers so skilled that Nico had recruited them from the FBI as part of his plans to modernize the centuries old business of organized crime.

Carmine's death was an execution. A message.

But Carlo Rossi was dead, and as far as Nico knew, there wasn't anyone loyal enough to him to seek revenge. Frank Morra had been Carlo's Consigliere, but Frank was even older than Carmine. More importantly, Frank was soft, apathetic. It was hard to imagine him even running the business in Carlo's absence, let alone planning a takedown of Nico, whose family had been the envy of the Syndicate until the mess with Angel and her father.

So who then? Who had both the motivation and ambition to come after the Vitale family so aggressively?

He thought about Dante. His former soldier had never worried him. He was a psychopath for sure — someone who'd had several run-ins with the law and more than one charge of violence against a woman. It was something Nico didn't tolerate in his organization, although he'd tried to be patient right up until Dante had put his hands on Angel. Then it had been over. He'd ordered a beating severe enough to send a message and banished Dante from the family for good.

He hadn't been surprised when Dante turned up working for Carlo, but was Dante smart enough and ambitious enough to attempt a takedown of the Vitale family? Could he rally the resources to follow him into this kind of battle? And if not Dante, then who? This kind of move took manpower. It took airtight loyalty. Who in the Syndicate could pull together all of those pieces in the few months since Carlo's death?

Frustrated all over again, he ran a hand through his hair and finished his drink, relishing the warmth of it on its way down his throat. He hated being exiled to the island on Maine, especially with Angel's ghost everywhere he looked. He had left only to give Luca and Vincent time to calm things down in New York, but he would be back soon enough. He would find out who had done this, and he would kill them.

He was contemplating the merit of another drink when he heard the hum of a boat. He held still, trying to get a read on its direction. Sound moved strangely across water, bouncing and bending in ways that made it difficult to pinpoint. The odds of anyone being out this far after dark were slim. Still, he couldn't afford to take any chances. He went inside to get his gun.

6

Ed left her on the beach where she'd arrived with Nico back in October. They'd been on the run from her father's men, and Angel had been torn between the part of her mind that told her to get away from the man who had kidnapped her, and the part that wanted nothing more than to be alone with Nico on his private island.

Now she couldn't deny the anticipation as she made her way through the woods with the flashlight Ed had given her. She told herself she just wanted to make sure Nico was okay. It didn't mean she'd forgiven him, didn't mean they could go anywhere from here.

But she would see him, at least.

The wind was gentle this time, different from the way it had been all those months ago when a storm had been brewing out over the Atlantic. It had stranded her and Nico here, giving them two precious days to be nothing but a man and a woman. It had been heaven and hell. A taste of what might have been if they were different people. A taste of what they could never be because they weren't.

She trudged forward through the forest, hoping she was heading in the right direction. She'd only ever made her way to the house with Nico, but she had a general sense of the island, and it wasn't that big. There were no other houses here, no other people. Worse case, she'd backtrack until she found it.

But backtracking wasn't necessary. Just when she was starting to think she was lost, she spilled out of the forest into a clearing. The house — all cedar shingles and glass and wraparound decks — seemed to hover at the top of a small hill.

The windows were dark, and she wondered if she was wrong, if Nico was somewhere else. But that didn't make sense. Ed wouldn't have brought her to the island if Nico wasn't here.

She used the flashlight to make her way up the gravel road toward the house. Her heart was pounding against her rib cage, although she didn't know if it was because she might be close to seeing Nico or because she was scared. What if the men who were after him had already found him? What if they were here, watching her from the house?

She walked a little slower, wondering for the first time if this was a good idea. Maybe she should have called Nico first, even if he told her not to come. But it didn't matter now; she was here, and there was no way back to the mainland without Ed. She picked up her pace, the reality of the situation solidifying her plans.

She was almost to the porch when she heard a voice from the shadows.

"How did you get here?"

She stopped, peering into the darkness in the direction of the voice. It took her a minute to see the shadow on the deck at the corner of the house. It took her another minute to find her own voice.

"Ed brought me. I waited for him on the dock."

"He shouldn't have done that," Nico said. She didn't know if it was anger or pain she heard in his voice. Maybe both.

"He's worried about you," she said. "So am I."

He sighed. "What are you doing here, Angel?"

"I heard about Carmine. I wanted to make sure you were okay."

Silence stretched between them, filled only with the sound of the waves rolling onto the beach below the house.

"I am."

She took a deep breath. She didn't know what she expected. That Nico would be happy to see her? That he would welcome her with open arms after she kicked him out of her life?

"Can I come inside so we can talk?" she asked.

For a minute she thought he might actually turn her away. Then he spoke again, his voice filled with a heavy kind of tiredness.

"Nowhere else to go tonight," he said. "Come in."

She stepped onto the porch and made her way toward the shadow. He came into view a little at a time, and she had to resist the urge to sigh when she finally saw his face. The chiseled line of his jaw, the sharp planes of his cheekbones under a shock of dark hair so lush, she had a sudden memory of it, silky and thick, in her fingers. But all of these were nothing compared to his eyes. In an instant, they pierced the armor she'd built over the past six months, and she was again prey to his predator.

Except now she was under no delusion that she wanted to escape. She almost forgot to breathe while she was held captive by his gaze. His body was mere inches from hers, and she caught his scent — raw masculinity, wool, and soap — on the ocean breeze.

He headed for the back of the house, then turned to look at her. "You coming?"

They entered through the glass doors off the living room. A fire burned in the hearth, and she had a flash of Nico, his naked body entwined with hers on the sofa while rain pelted the windows.

She forced her eyes away from the fireplace, taking in the sweep of wood floor, the stone walls, the glass that made the ocean feel like it was part of the house. She'd forgotten how much she loved this place, how at home she'd felt here.

Nico reached for her bag, and a shock of desire winged through her body as his hand brushed against her cold fingers. He set the bag on the ground and crossed the room to pull a blanket off the back of the sofa. She watched as he made his way toward her, his eyes locked on hers while he leaned in to wrap the blanket around her shoulders. She hadn't realized she was shivering until the warmth settled over her skin. He let his hands rest on her arms for a moment before turning away, and she exhaled a breath she hadn't realized she'd been holding.

She had forgotten how hard it was to breathe around him, as if he was a force so powerful, he consumed every ounce of oxygen in the air.

"Drink?" he asked, already heading for the bar.

"Please."

He poured something into a glass and returned to hand it to her.

"Thank you."

He nodded, and gestured at the couch. "Sit."

She took a seat on the sofa and felt the sting of rejection when he sat at the other end. Complicated was an understatement for everything that was between them, but she couldn't deny that all the old feelings were still there. Was it simpler for him? Had his feelings for her changed?

"How are you?" he finally asked.

She took a drink, then looked down at the whiskey in her glass. "I'm… okay. Still getting used to everything the way it is now."

"And David?"

She looked up, surprised that he would mention her brother. "He's okay, too," she said softly. "Dealing with all the unfinished business between him and our father."

"I'm sure that's very difficult," Nico said, his voice full of regret.

She nodded, then took a deep breath. "I'm sorry about Carmine."

"Thank you."

She looked into his eyes. "What's going on, Nico?"

"I thought you might know," he said.

"Me?" She shook her head. "I'm not involved in the Boston operation, but I doubt Frank has the ambition to come after you."

"I thought the same thing," he said.

"Besides," she said, "why would someone kill Carmine? Wasn't he just a Consigliere?"

She was still learning the terminology of her father's illegal businesses, but she knew that Carmine had been a kind of advisor to Nico, the same way Frank had advised her father. Consigliere's weren't supposed to be part of the battlefield.

"I'm not sure I would use the word "just" to describe Carmine — or anyone in that role."

"You know what I mean." It came out sharper than she intended. She didn't know much about the business, but she wasn't stupid.

She thought she saw a flash of appreciation in his eyes. Figures. Nico wasn't the kind of man to be turned on by complacency, however much he might have railed against her stubbornness.

"I do," he said. "And you're right. Someone in Carmine's position isn't usually a target for this kind of message."

The whiskey and blanket conspired to make her more comfortable than she should have been, and she let the blanket slip off her shoulders. "What kind of message is it?"

"If I had to guess, I'd say it was designed to remind me that my allies are rapidly decreasing in number."

"Why would someone want to do that?" she asked.

"I don't know," he said. "There could be a hundred reasons."

She thought about it. "If why isn't the place to start, how about who?"

"If I knew that," he said, "I wouldn't be sitting here."

There was something ferocious in his voice, and she knew it was true; if Nico knew who had done this to him, to Carmine, that person would be dead.

"What about Dante?" she asked. "Could he be involved?"

"I don't know," he said.

"Is there anyone else you can think of who would want to hurt you?"

A smile touched the corners of his lips. "There are a lot of people who want to hurt me."

She took a drink of the whiskey, savoring the way it seeped into her system. Already everything seemed a little less intense. Nico was so close. It would be nothing to cross the space between them, to take his face in her hands and touch her lips to his.

"What are you going to do?" she asked.

He stood, then walked to her end of the couch. "I'm going to go to bed."

He held out his hand.

7

He pulled her to her feet, their bodies so close she could feel the raw power of him, like a planet with a gravitational pull she was powerless to resist. He took her glass and set it on the coffee table before leading her out of the living room.

They ascended the stairs to the second floor where Angel followed him into the master bedroom. The doors were open to the second floor balcony, and the curtains billowed in the breeze, the salty scent of the sea filling the room. A fire had started between her legs, and she was finding it difficult to get the air in and out of her lungs.

She thought he would lead her to the bed, but he headed for the bathroom instead. When they got there, he released her hand and turned on the shower. He looked down at her as the room filled with steam, then snaked his big hands around her neck until he was cupping her face. He rubbed his thumb over her bottom lip in a familiar gesture that sent a lick of heat to her center. She opened her mouth, capturing his finger and sucking until his eyes turned dark with desire.

The room was invisible around them, the steam swirling like fog off the water. He bent his head to hers.

"Angel…" He breathed her name just before he covered her lips with his own.

She melted into the familiar contours of his muscled body, molding her softness to every sculpted plane as he fit his mouth to hers, sweeping and exploring like it was the first time he'd tasted her. She opened to him like no time had passed, like there was nothing in the world but the soft, urgent stroke of his tongue stoking the fires of her desire.

He was already hard for her, his cock straining against the fabric of his jeans. There was an answering wetness at her core, and she ran her hands across his chest, down the flat plane of his stomach, over the bulge between his legs. She cupped him through his jeans and felt him grow harder, bigger.

He groaned and stepped away, pulling off her shirt, unhooking her bra, sliding her pants down until she was standing bare before him. He looked at her for a long moment, his breath hitching before he took off his own clothes, revealing his chiseled body in all its perfection.

When they were both naked, he led her into the shower. For a moment, he held her against him, letting the water rush over their bodies. It was a kind of cleansing, a washing away of the outside world and everything that was between them. Then his hands were everywhere, cupping the fullness of her breasts, tracing the curve of her waist as it flared into her hips, lifting her ass until she was pressed against every inch of his rigid manhood.

Their bodies were wet and slippery, the sensation erotic and sensual as his tongue invaded her mouth, his slick hardness a tortuous contrast to the softness of her own body. She ached for him, and the beating between her legs grew to a fever pitch as his satin tip pressed against her belly. She knew exactly how he would feel driving into her, knew that it was the only answer to the question pulsing in her wet heat.

She moved her hands over his chest, pinching his nipples until he gasped, then continued down to his chiseled abs. He was breathing fast, his cock pushing against her stomach by the time she wrapped her fingers around him.

He took her face in his hands. "Why did you have to come back?"

She wasn't insulted. There was so much pain in the words. She understood him perfectly; they'd gotten used to the torture of being apart. How would they do it now that they had been forced to remember? How could they deny everything they felt, chalk it up to the heat of the moment, to extraordinary circumstances, when the proof was the inferno building between them?

"I don't know how I stayed away," she murmured.

He lowered his head, groaning into her mouth while she stroked him. He got bigger and harder, and her own arousal grew as her body begged for him to fill her. Finally he moved her hand away and guided her to the wall of the shower. He took their kiss deeper, his tongue pillaging her mouth in a way that was too reminiscent of the way he took command of her body when he was fucking her. An explosion was building deep inside the folds of her sex, the orgasm teasing her with its promise. He turned her around, placing her hands on the shower wall.

"Don't move," he ordered, his voice gruff.

He disappeared, then moved behind her, his tip brushing against her ass.

She pressed back into him, out of her mind with need. There was nothing but him, his hands on her hips, his muscled thighs behind hers as he positioned the head of his shaft at her entrance, his cock poised to push inside her.

"Nico, please... Now..."

She was deep in the abyss of her desire for him, the place where nothing else existed and nothing else mattered but feeling him complete her. He leaned over her back, his mouth at her ear.

"Now?"

She rotated her hips against him. "Yes... I can't... I can't stand it. I need you."

He growled, and a moment later he was inside of her with one, deep thrust.

The water spilled over her back as he took her. There was nothing tender about it. This was about urgency, about ownership. He took her with a savagery that stole her breath, holding her hips and bringing her body back to meet his thrusts until she cried out with the pleasure-pain of it. She didn't want it to stop — ever — and she opened herself to him, wanting him deeper, harder.

He reached around her body and rubbed his thumb against her clit, and her body blossomed like a long dead flower in spring.

"Come for me, baby."

The words sparked the fire in her pussy, and she felt herself closing in on the top of the peak that was never far when Nico was inside of her.

She looked over her shoulder at him. "Come with me."

He groaned as he buried himself inside her, the tip of his shaft hitting the most secret part of her body as his fingers worked in concert to bring her closer to climax, the edge of the universe in sight. Then she was over it, flying through the abyss, breaking apart like an ancient star while the orgasm rocked through her body and Nico shuddered with an anguished growl.

She lay limp against the shower wall, barely able to hold herself upright while Nico panted behind her, his hands still on her hips. He left kisses in the water streaming down her back, then turned her around, ferociously plundering her mouth like he needed to prove to himself that she was real.

When they'd both caught their breath, Nico turned off the water and came back with a towel. After they dried off, Nico took her hand and led her to the bed. He pulled her down next to him, holding her naked body against his as the waves rushed onto the beach below the house. There was too much to say and not nearly enough. She let herself fall into the rhythm of his heartbeat, as familiar as a lullaby. It was the last thing she remembered before she tumbled into the void of sleep.

8

He lay in bed for a long time after he woke up, trying to memorize the feel of her against him. He'd been surprised to see her walking toward the house, had been both desperate and afraid to see her. He'd learned to live without her, if that's what you could call what he'd been doing. It hadn't been easy, but he'd been doing it, had taught himself to tiptoe around her memory when it had the most power to harm him. Now she was back, and he felt anew the all-consuming need for her. It was beyond physical, although he wouldn't fool himself into believing she wasn't made for him, that her body wasn't created as a perfect match to his.

But it wasn't only that. It was something more elemental, something that went beyond flesh and bone. His soul knew hers, had experienced a visceral jolt of recognition the first time he'd seen her. It was ridiculous and fanciful, not at all in line with the practicality he'd honed to a fine point in the name of running the Vitale empire. Knowing when to reward, when to threaten, when to kill… those things were easy compared to the mysterious chemical attraction he had to Angel Rossi.

Did she go by Rossi now? Or had she stuck with Bondesan in the wake of her father's death? He wouldn't blame her if she had. Carlo Rossi had been one of the worst of the Syndicate's bosses, had held his own daughter at gunpoint to try and escape Nico in London. He didn't deserve to have her carry on his name.

Sunlight was leaking through the windows when he finally slid out from under her arm. He didn't want to do it, would have stayed in bed with her all day if he could. But his business — and the only family he had left — was under threat. He couldn't afford to be emotional at their expense.

He pulled on a pair of sweats and left the room, then descended the stairs to the kitchen. He dialed Luca's number while he started the coffee.

Luca picked up on the first ring. "Boss."

"Talk," Nico said into the phone.

"Are you okay?" Luca asked.

"No," Nico said. "I'm not okay. I'm hiding like some kind of pussy while someone targets my business."

"Got it," Luca said, his voice tight.

"I don't care if you have it," Nico said. "What are you doing about it?"

"We've put out the word, and we're leaning hard on every informant we have, anyone who has an ear to the ground with the Syndicate, to try and figure out who's behind Carmine's murder."

"And?" Nico prompted.

Luca exhaled. "It's not much. Sara said the data breach looks like it originated in LA. Took her awhile to find it. Apparently it was routed through several other IPs in Asia."

"LA?" Nico couldn't hide his surprise. "That's... unexpected..."

"I thought the same thing," Luca said.

"I'll call John, feel him out."

John Lando was head of the west coast family, and while they were part of the Syndicate, John was a breed all his own. Born and bred in Los Angeles, the movie business was a big portion of John's legitimate income stream. The man had a love for film that was unrivaled, and Nico often suspected he only bothered to run the illegal portion of his business to fund the movies that were so near and dear to his heart. John was Sinatra to Farrell Black's commando, and he had never made secret the fact that he found the more violent aspects of the Syndicate distasteful. He usually stayed on the sidelines during Syndicate scuffles and turf wars.

"Want me to do it?" Luca asked.

"No. I'll take care of it."

"Okay, but we should meet," Luca said. "We need to figure out a game plan."

"That's a given. I have no intention of sitting on my ass, waiting for these bastards to finish the job they started."

"Well, don't come here," Luca said. "It's a fucking madhouse."

"Exactly why I'm coming back tonight. I'm not going to leave the men exposed while I play it safe."

"Whoever's doing this is after you. The business, Carmine, the shipments… they were all just a means to an end. If you want to protect the family, you'll steer clear of Headquarters until we get this figured out."

"I need to pay my respect to Carmine's family," Nico said. "I've known them my whole life."

Luca lowered his voice, like he didn't want anyone around him to hear what he was saying. "That is not a good idea. And I've already talked to Mary. She understands."

Mary was Carmine's wife of four decades.

"That may be," Nico said. "But I'm not a coward, and I won't hide from these people, whoever they are."

"Nico - "

"I have some arrangements to make," Nico said, cutting him off. "I'll call you later with the details."

He hung up before Luca could say anything else. He meant well, but whoever had targeted the Vitale family intended to drive Nico underground. He'd be damned if he gave them the satisfaction of succeeding.

A glance at his phone told him it was only eight am. Plenty of time for a run to clear his head. He went to the entryway and pulled on his shoes, then slipped out the front door, and started down the gravel road.

The morning air was cool and wet, with the promise of heat that was only present a few months out of the year in Maine. He made his way through the trees — slowly coming back to life after the long winter — and headed for the beach, then turned right to run parallel to the water.

The island was his sacred space, even more so since the two days he'd spent here with Angel. No one knew about the hideaway, not even Luca. It was the place Nico came when he needed a break from the weight of the responsibility on his shoulders, a place where nature could remind him how insignificant he really was. It was comforting, and he'd found himself stealing away more often since the shootout with Angel's father, trying to quiet the churning of his mind and the questions that seemed to have no answers.

Questions like: did the Syndicate and its businesses add any value at all to the world at large? Was the little good he managed to do worth all the death and destruction? And most importantly of all, was he really a businessman? Or was the price of his suit the only difference between him and the criminals shoved every day into the back of police cars?

He pushed himself to run harder and faster over the rocks that jutted out over the water. It was a test of his concentration and agility, and for a few moments he didn't have space in his mind for anything but running without breaking his neck.

When he returned to the sand, he circled back toward the house. Angel was there, waiting for him, maybe still in bed, her long hair spread across his pillow. He felt a stirring in his blood at the thought of her naked body sprawled across his sheets, and his feet moved faster of their own accord.

He passed by the front door and continued onto the deck, following it to the back of the house. The glass doors were open, Angel standing with her back to him while she cut oranges on the countertop. He leaned against the door jamb, wanting to soak her in, remember the way she looked in all the moments to come when they wouldn't be together.

Her hair was piled on top of her head, loose tendrils tickling the collar of the shirt — his shirt — that hit the top of her bare thighs. He was immediately hard, wondering if she was naked underneath it, if he could come up behind her, snake his arms around her waist, be inside of her in seconds.

She was humming softly to herself while she placed the oranges into the juicer, her slender arms working as she pressed down on the handle. The sleeves on the shirt were too long, and she'd haphazardly rolled them up to keep them out of her way. Catching her this way, unselfconscious and innocent, was strangely endearing, and a familiar wave of protectiveness washed over him.

He didn't want her back in his world. It was vile and dirty and dangerous and violent.

Everything she wasn't.

There was nothing for her with him. Nothing but death and fear, and she deserved better than that. Deserved better than him.

Which is why she would have to go.

9

She was turning to rinse her hands in the sink when she caught sight of him in the doorway.

She jumped a little. "You scared me."

His lips curved up in the slight smile she loved so much. It was a smile that said he had a secret or three. A smile that was meant only for her.

"I'm sorry," he said, his voice hoarse. "I never want you to be scared, least of all with me."

She looked at him for a long minute; the well-formed chest, bare over sweatpants that should have made him look sloppy but instead made him as alluring as ever. The shock of dark hair falling over his forehead. The sweep of eyelashes, so dark and long they would make any woman envious. There was some color in his cheeks, and she suddenly saw him as he must have looked when he a boy. The image caused an unfamiliar hitch in her chest, a moment of loss that cut her to the bone even though he was standing right in front of her.

She rinsed her hands, then grabbed a dishtowel and dried them as she crossed the room. She draped the towel over one of her shoulders and reached up to wrap her arms around his neck, surprised to realize he was already hard for her. She pressed against him, stretching on tiptoe to touch her lips to his. He groaned when she slipped her tongue into his mouth.

She pulled away to look at him. "Where were you?"

He grabbed her hips, tugged her back against him. "Running."

She raised an eyebrow. "Running? I could have come up with some physical activity if you'd wanted the exercise."

He growled, squeezing her ass until she could feel his shaft against her belly.

She laughed, turning away as he grabbed the towel and swatted her ass with it. "Hungry?" she asked him.

"I'm hungry, all right."

His voice was dangerously low, and she couldn't hide the grin that rose to her face. "Me, too. But first, we eat breakfast."

She'd been conflicted the last time they'd been together — and understandably so. She was still conflicted about a lot of things, but not about her feelings for Nico. They were as obvious and undeniable as the sea that surrounded the island. The time would come for them to talk about what was next, but not yet. This was the place where they could be together with no ugliness between them. She wouldn't worry about the future until she had to.

She made bacon and eggs from the store of food in the fridge, then set the table, all under Nico's voracious gaze. She thought he might devour her whole before they ever got to breakfast, and she had to fight against the tide of her own desire as she moved around him. She was like a moth to a flame; she knew he was dangerous, that her feelings for him were dangerous. But he was so mesmerizing she couldn't seem to stop herself from dancing gleefully around the fire.

They sat close at the table. He covered one of her bare feet with his own while they ate, like he couldn't bear not to touch her for even a minute. They talked about the island, about the massive snow storm that had landed when he'd been there over Christmas. It caught her off guard, and she had to fight to keep her face impassive. Nico wouldn't want her pity, but the thought of him alone on their island at Christmas opened up a floodgate of sadness inside her. The holidays had been rough in the wake of her father's death and the loss of Nico, but at least she'd had David. For all of Nico's power and authority and wealth, he might be the loneliest person in the world. In spite of everything, she thought that he deserved better.

They took a shower and got dressed, then headed outside, walking the same path they'd traveled last October when lightning had ripped the sky and the rain had fallen in sheets. Now the sun was high overhead, a mild breeze drifting in from the water. They walked mostly in silence, and she thrilled at the feel of his big hand over hers. For the first time in six months, she felt complete. Her father's death and everything that had happened in London seemed a million miles away. She didn't even know how she felt about it anymore. Had she come to the place where she could forgive Nico? Where she could give him the benefit of the doubt about his motives, believing that he'd killed her father to protect her and not to exact vengeance for the death of his own parents?

She didn't know, and she didn't know if she'd ever have a chance to find out. They were back in crisis mode, trying to survive with minimal collateral damage. It was impossible to think about the future and what it held for them, impossible to even fathom what it might look like. She knew she didn't want to be part of his world — part of the world her father had occupied. But could he be part of hers? Could he be a regular man? She tried to imagine him heading off to work at MediaComm, the business he owned that operated as a front for the illegal income streams that were part of the Syndicate. Nico waking up and heading into the office every day? Home in time for dinner? Little League games on the weekend?

It was impossible.

Nico was a different breed of man. A man who would kill to protect what was his. A man who had.

Life with him wouldn't be normal, and normal had been all she ever wanted.

"What are you thinking about?" he asked, dropping a kiss on her head.

They were heading back toward the house, working their way along the beach until they had to cut through the trees.

She leaned against his arm and laughed a little. "You don't want to know."

She felt him sigh. He knew what she was thinking about without a word between them. "It's unavoidable."

"I know."

They continued to the house and made their way up the rear deck to the living room. She poured a glass of water from the tap, bracing herself for the words Nico would say. She could feel them hanging in the air, heavy with unspoken significance.

"Angel."

His voice was quiet behind her, and when she turned around, he was leaning against the counter, his big arms crossed over his chest.

"Let me help." The words were out of her mouth before she could even think about them.

A ghost of a smile touched his lips. "No."

"Nico - "

He cut her off. "There's nothing you can do."

"You don't know that," she said. "I have access to the Rossi family, to people there who might have information on what's happening."

"They won't talk to you, Angel. And even if they would, I wouldn't want them to."

"If you're trying to protect me, it's too late." She heard the bitterness in her voice and immediately regretted the words. It was a low blow. She knew Nico was sorry for what had happened in London.

He didn't flinch, but she saw his anger in the hard set of his jaw, the flinty shine in his eyes. "I'm just getting started," he said. "I may not have been able to protect you before, but I can do it now."

"It's not your decision."

"The hell it's not." It came out as a shout.

"You don't control me, Nico. You tried that before, remember?"

"I do remember," he said, his voice flat. "And look what happened."

She felt the words like a punch to the gut. "So what happened in London is my fault."

"I'm not saying that, Angel. You know I'm not. But I tried to protect you then, to keep you out of whatever was coming."

"Well, I'm sorry if I couldn't sit back and have my nails done while you confronted my father about whether or not he killed your parents."

He stepped toward her, placing his hands on her arms. "That's not what I expect of you, and you know it. This business is ugly. Why do you want to be involved?"

"Do you have to ask?" She looked away, not wanting to meet his eyes. She might fall in, never to return, and then Nico would have his way, like always.

"Angel." She didn't turn back to him. Couldn't. "Look at me."

She did then, because she could never resist the pull of his voice, his eyes.

"I love you. I think it's been true since that first night in my apartment. You were so scared and stubborn and brave. I'd never seen anything more beautiful. Still haven't. Don't you get it?"

"Get what?"

"Someone is waging war on me, on everything and everyone that matters to me." He lowered his mouth to hers, branded her with a firm, chaste kiss that set her body on fire. "And no one matters more than you."

"It's not your decision." It was hard to say the words again. Not because it wasn't true or because she was afraid of him — she knew he would never hurt her. It was hard because she wanted to make things easy for him, wanted to be the one thing he didn't have to carry on his broad shoulders. But she couldn't. She couldn't just sit in the background while Nico was in danger. Couldn't go back to her quiet life knowing that he was under attack.

He sighed, dropping his hands from her shoulders. "It is. I have to meet up with Luca. You can stay here or you can go home, but you're not coming with me."

"Then I'll go to Headquarters and see what I can find out on my own. But first I'll stop in Boston and talk to Frank Morra."

"You will not do either of those things," he said through clenched teeth.

"You can't stop me." She felt childish saying it, but it was true. She was a grown woman. She could do what she wanted, and she wanted to help him.

He turned away from her with an exasperated sigh and walked to the deck. She watched him from inside the house as he placed his hands on the railing. She wanted to hold firm, to wait for him to give in, but she couldn't stand to see him so tortured over her safety.

She walked outside and wrapped her arms around his waist, rested her head on his powerful back. She stood still, waiting for him to soften toward her. When she felt his body loosen, she moved in front of him and reached up to touch his face.

"Let me do this, Nico. No one's watching me. I can move freely, and I can do some digging with Frank, see if he lets something slip that might help." She continued in a rush, encouraged by his silence. "I'll do whatever you say, I promise."

"Except leave it to me," he said quietly.

"Except that." She kissed him gently on the lips, then looked into his eyes. "I don't know where this is going, what kind of future we have, but I know you wouldn't leave me alone if I needed help. I'm not leaving you either. You can't ask that of me, Nico. Not when you wouldn't do it."

She saw the defeat in his eyes even before he nodded.

"But you do what I say as if your life depends on it," he said, his eyes piercing hers. "Because it might."

10

They made love long into the night, Nico staking claim to her body all over again, mapping her with his hands, charting new courses over every curve, in every fold. Then there was no Syndicate. No assassinations or violence. There was only Nico's strong hands on her skin, bending her to his will, invading her body with his own until it seemed they had always been one.

The next morning, they left Nico's car with Ed and took Angel's little Honda down 195 to Boston. Nico filled her in on everything that had happened within the Vitale family — the interrupted shipments, the defection of his soldiers, the physical violence perpetrated against his men. Alone, the incidents could have been chalked up to the kind of random interruptions that occurred in every business. Together the problems pointed to an obvious threat against Nico and his interests.

Not too long ago, her father would have been the first suspect. But he was dead and buried, and Angel had no idea who would have both the motive and the resources to launch such an aggressive attack. She didn't love being back in close proximity to the Syndicate, but she meant what she said to Nico — she couldn't return to her safe, quiet life while he was in danger. She would try to help, and then she would retreat from this world for good.

She'd never felt an attachment to Boston — she and David had been exiled to boarding school almost immediately following their mother's death and had rarely returned home afterward — but the sight of it rising up near the water brought an unexpected wave of grief. This had been home once, and whenever she'd thought of her father, she had imagined him here. She and David had only been back a couple of times since the funeral, but she'd been too preoccupied with the work of going through the house to dwell on any residual affection she might have for the city. Now she realized there was nothing keeping her tied to it. She could go anywhere, start over, do anything. She wondered why the thought didn't bring her the relief she expected.

They pulled into a parking garage near the business district. Nico's brow was furrowed with worry as they exited onto Boylston Street, and Angel took his hand, pulling him out of the stream of suited men and women traversing the sidewalks.

She reached up, put her hands on either side of his face. "Hey."

He looked down at her without saying anything, his face stony.

"I'll be fine," she said. "This isn't enemy territory for me." She tried for a lighthearted grin. "I kind of own the place, you know."

He didn't smile. Instead, he pointed to a sandwich shop across the street. "I'll be right there," he said. "If you're not back in an hour, I'm coming in after you."

She had to resist the urge to shudder. The day Nico stepped into the enemy territory of Rossi Development was the day all hell would break loose. Because Nico wouldn't come in politely asking for her. He'd come in shooting, and he wouldn't leave until he had her.

"Don't do that," she said, even though she knew it wouldn't do any good. "I'll do my best to be back in an hour, but I don't want it to seem like I just stopped in to pump Frank for information. Just… trust me, Nico. I've got this."

She touched her lips to his and turned for the glass and steel skyscraper that was headquarters to her father's legitimate — and unbeknownst to most people, illegitimate — business interests. She felt Nico's eyes on her, but she didn't look back. It would only make things worse for him.

She entered the marble lobby of the Prudential Tower and showed her ID to the security guard at the front desk. After they confirmed with someone upstairs that she had permission to be there, she took the elevator to the forty-eighth floor. Frank was waiting for her, a wide smile plastered on his face, when she stepped into the company lobby.

"Angelica!" he said, his voice an octave too loud. "What a nice surprise."

"Hi, Uncle Frank."

The words almost got stuck in her throat, and her smile felt painted on. Frank Morra had been a fixture in her life since birth, but she'd had no idea that he was part of the Boston Syndicate until Nico had kidnapped her. Seeing him spun a complex web of emotion in her brain — nostalgia and memory and disgust and bitterness all intertwined into something she couldn't begin to sort.

She caught the scent of his imported cigarettes as he put an arm around her shoulders. "To what do we owe this honor? Are you in town with friends?"

Her face heated with annoyance. Is that what he thought of her? That she was some carefree twenty-something with nothing better to do than party?

"I'm here to see my father's office."

She saw him try to hide his surprise in the moment before he donned the trusty grin. "Why would you want to do that, honey? There's nothing in there for you. It will just bring up bad memories."

Like almost everyone, Frank was under the impression that Angel had been caught in the crossfire between Nico — the man who kidnapped her — and her father. He knew that she'd finally been exposed to her father's other business interests, but that was as far as it went. That was fine. She would use his condescension in her favor.

"I need to see it, Uncle Frank." She tried for an expression of grief-stricken angst. "I just do."

He nodded somberly. "I understand. They say closure is important in these things."

She didn't know who "they" were, but she nodded anyway.

"Come on." He guided her past the receptionist toward a long, carpeted hallway. "How are you? How is David?"

"We're getting by."

There had been a time when Frank Morra had been as familiar to her as her own father, but she hadn't really known him at all. She'd done a lot of reading on the Rossi crime empire since she'd returned from London, and while the extent of her father's illegal dealings was murky to law enforcement, one thing was clear; whatever her father had been involved in, Frank Morra had been right alongside him. And that made him every bit as responsible for the reprehensible things her father had done. She and David would have to do something about him — about everything.

They worked their way to the back of the giant office space and a shorter, more luxurious hall. Angel had a flash of memory; holding her mother's hand, looking up at the carved wooden doors and the gold plaques that lined the hallway, David skipping along beside them.

"I'm acting as interim Chairman, as you know," Frank said as they approached the double doors at the end of the hall, "but it doesn't feel right to do anything with your father's belongings before someone permanent is appointed to the position. His office is just as he left it."

"I appreciate that," she said, although really, she couldn't have cared less about her father's things.

Frank opened the doors, and Angel's eyes swept the expanse of lush gray carpet and modern furniture, the sunlight muted through the walls of tinted glass at the other end of the room.

"Can I have Theresa get you something?" Frank asked. "Water? Scotch?"

She shook her head. "I'd just like to be alone for a bit."

He squeezed her shoulder. "I understand, honey. We're all here for you if you need anything. Don't forget to say goodbye before you leave. I'm right next door."

He stepped into the hallway, and she wondered if he'd left the door open intentionally.

It didn't matter. This was her company now.

She shut the door and crossed to the big windows. The vantage point was expansive, looking out over the city and beyond to a sliver of the harbor. How many times had her father stood here, looking at this very same view? How much of the city's crime was a result of the businesses he had run from this room? How many people had been hurt?

Her stomach turned over at the thought, and she spun around to face the room. She didn't have time to agonize over the choices her father had made, to look behind her. There was only forward motion now. Help Nico. Dismantle her father's business with the Syndicate. Get rid of Rossi Development. Move on.

In that order.

She studied the room, then moved toward the big cabinet that sat against one wall. She started with the cupboard doors that fronted the piece, opening them quietly in case Frank could hear her next door in his office. But the cabinet didn't tell her anything other than the fact that her father liked to drink; there was a set of barware, enough liquor to host a party, several crystal drinking glasses, and a box of cigars. She closed the cupboard doors and started with the drawers on either side.

Empty except for a stack of clean white shirts in one of them.

Pulling her phone from her pocket, she checked the time and guessed that she had about fifteen more minutes before Frank came to check on her. The realization got her moving, and she hurried across the room to the desk, a streamlined design of right angles and light wood anchored with slim white panels.

The surface of the desk was virtually clean. There was a leather blotter, a metal cup full of pens and pencils, a picture of her mother. Had someone cleaned it, or had her father always been this neat? And what had happened to his computer? Would asking about it make Frank suspicious?

She opened the top drawer of the desk and was disappointed to find it empty. A quick check of two more drawers revealed only a few pieces of company letterhead, an old pair of eyeglasses (she hadn't known her father wore glasses), and a dop kit with a razor, shaving cream, and saline solution. She had already resigned herself to coming up empty when she opened the last drawer.

Her nose was immediately assaulted by the smell of cigarettes. She reached into the back of the drawer and closed her hand around something cold and flat. When she pulled it out she saw that it was an ashtray, loaded with cigarette butts. She knew immediately that they belonged to Frank — the cigarettes he smoked gave off a uniquely unpleasant odor — but she lifted the glass dish to her nose anyway.

A million memories came rushing back; Uncle Frank lifting her into the air on her fifth birthday, putting her on his shoulders so she could see during the St. Patrick's Day parade downtown, teasing her with gifts by switching hands behind his back.

She leaned back in the chair. It didn't mean anything. Frank Morra had known her father most of their lives. He'd probably just come in here to think about his dead friend, to think about the business.

But something nagged at her. Frank had made it sound like the office was waiting for the next Chairman of Rossi Development while making it seem like he wasn't interested in the job. Was it an act? Did he sit in her father's office, dreaming about taking over?

The truth is, she didn't really care. It was more about the deceit. About the part Frank played, the one where he was the grieving best friend of Carlo Rossi, determined to see to his legacy, not interested in building one of his own. If he was lying, it meant that he was more ambitious — and maybe more intelligent — than Nico gave him credit for.

She set the ashtray on top of the desk and felt around the back of the drawer. She didn't expect to find anything else. The cigarettes weren't exactly incriminating. But then her fingers brushed against something thin and dry at the back of the drawer. She pulled it out, and realized she was looking at a folded piece of paper. When she smoothed it out, she saw that it was a sheet of company letterhead, STRAND SOUTH BAY, written in neat block letters across its surface.

"Strand," she murmured.

She glanced quickly at her phone and thought about Nico at the cafe across the street. She didn't doubt for a second that he'd make good on his promise to come in after her, and it been almost an hour since she'd left him on the sidewalk outside. She needed to get moving,

She folded the piece of paper and returned it to the drawer where she found it. If it did belong to Frank, she didn't want him to know she'd found it. Then she put the ash tray back and closed the drawer. She was preparing to leave the room when the door opened.

Frank entered the room, all smiles. Was it her imagination that he seemed nervous?

"How are you doing in here?" he asked.

"I'm fine." She didn't bother with the grief-stricken daughter act. She'd gotten access to her father's office. Frank would either let something slip or he wouldn't.

"Good, good," he said. "You hungry? Want to grab some food?"

She shook her head. "I can't. I have an appointment."

He looked relieved. "I'm sorry to hear that. Next time then."

"Sure."

"I'll walk you out," he said, taking her elbow and propelling her out the door.

She waited until they hit the lobby to face him. "What's going on with the Vitale family?"

A look of panic crossed Frank's face before he recovered. It was all she needed to see.

"What do you mean?"

He was stalling for time, but it didn't matter. He wouldn't tell her anything, but now she was sure that he knew something about what was going on.

"I heard about Carmine," she said.

He almost sighed with relief. Carmine's murder had been splashed all over the news. Her knowledge of it didn't imply any kind of contact or sympathy with Nico.

"I don't know about that." He looked around, then lowered his voice. "But we shouldn't be talking about that kind of business here."

She nodded.

"Is there anything I can do for you?" he asked.

She met his watery gaze. "I think I have everything I need."

He shuffled a little on his feet, like he was unnerved by her stare. "Glad to hear it. Just let me know if you think of anything."

"I will." She headed for the elevator, than remembered something and turned around to look at him. "Actually, there is one thing."

He smiled. "Anything."

"Make sure the security guards downstairs know I'm not a visitor. After all, I own this company now."

11

Nico was still on edge when they landed in Miami later that day. It had taken every ounce of his self-control to stay in the cafe across the street while Angel went inside alone. He'd killed some time calling John Lando in LA, trying to feel him out for information about the uprising against him. But John had been distracted and unhelpful, and Nico couldn't tell if it was because he really didn't know anything, or because he was hiding something. Nico had spent the rest of the time watching the clock, more than willing to go in after Angel if she didn't return in time.

But she had, safe and sound, and he'd been surprised by the resolute set of her spine, the stubborn lift of her chin. She even looked a little pissed. She hadn't gotten anything but a piece of paper with a couple of words on it, but Frank's reaction had made her almost certain he knew something about what was going on.

It wasn't good news for Nico. It meant the conspiracy against him was probably bigger than one person, or at the very least, was being allowed by other members of the family. He revisited everything that had happened, wondering again if Carmine and Raneiro had been right. Had Nico's reorganization of the family proven too much for the old world mentality of the men who had been a part of it for generations? Was the added income too small an upside for business strategies that might have seemed soft to men who had made their living wielding power through brutality?

Or had he lost their respect when he'd spared Angel? When he'd revealed his weakness for her by keeping her safe and killing her father?

He knew there were people in the family who supported him, but they were young, mostly members of his own generation. He'd tried to pave the way for the older members to retire in comfort, but it was impossible to know if they'd left with their dignity intact. And then there were the others. Members of the family for whom age wasn't an excuse.

Like Dante Santoro, who simply liked violence for the sake of it.

He looked down at Angel as they walked through the airport. She was as beautiful as ever in a sundress with slim straps, her hair falling in waves around her shoulders. He would kill without hesitation to protect her, and yet here she was, drawn back into the web of danger because of him.

"Should we catch a cab?" she asked when they stepped out into the sticky, heavy heat of Miami.

He took her elbow. "No cab."

"But - "

"I've got it under control." He guided her to short term parking and scanned the lot until he found what he was looking for. Then he led her toward the sleek, red machine crouched in the shadows.

She narrowed her eyes. "What is this?"

"This is a car," Nico said. He reached under the wheel well and withdrew a set of keys. A high pitched beep echoed through the garage, and the doors opened out and up, flanking the car like wings. "An F150 LaFerrari , to be exact. Now get in."

12

The car was more animal than machine, its undulating curves sensual even rendered in steel and fiberglass. She shouldn't have been surprised. Nico was all man — not exactly the type to drive a low-key sedan — and this car wasn't about subtlety.

"Shouldn't we be laying low?" she asked.

"We are laying low," he said. "I had someone change the plates."

She raised an eyebrow. "Someone? I thought the point of meeting Luca here was to stay under the radar."

"Trust me. I've covered our bases. And when in Rome…" He took her elbow and guided her to the car.

"We're not in Rome," she said drily.

"No, we're in Miami. Let's go."

She slid into the seat with a sigh, sinking into the plush leather interior. He reached across her and buckled her seatbelt, just like he had the night they'd fled New York for Maine. His touch was no less electric now, and she breathed in the scent of him as his fingers brushed her skin, imagining the way he laid his big hands across her naked belly just before he spread her legs to enter her.

He clicked the buckle into place and retreated from the car. A moment later her door slid shut with a quiet hum. He got behind the wheel, and the powerful engine came to life somewhere between a roar and purr.

Like Nico.

He put his hands on the wheel slowly, like he was savoring the feel of it under his hands. He shifted into gear, and then they were flying through the parking garage, Nico taking the turns sharp and smooth until they exited into the Florida sunshine.

They got on the highway and headed south. It was like being in a different world, the bright colors and fast cars standing in sharp contrast to the wild Maine coast, the historical solemnity of Boston. Nico rolled down the windows and looked over at her with a grin, then accelerated through traffic. The wind whipped back her hair, and she was surprised to hear laughter bubble up from her throat.

She wasn't a car person, couldn't have cared less what she drove at home, but the speed and agility of the machine connected with something deeply erotic inside her. She looked over at Nico — his muscled thighs moving as he shifted gears, dark hair ruffled by the wind, eyes hidden behind sunglasses — and grew wet with desire for him. She felt her old life falling away with a startling lack of fear.

A half hour later, Nico pulled into the Coral Gables address Angel had given him. The house was one of many owned by her father — now owned by her and David — and occupied only sporadically. It wasn't one of her favorites — she'd always thought it was a little garish — but now she appreciated the gated entry, the long driveway that led to a brick courtyard at the front of the house. The house wasn't a fortress — as far as she knew it had been built for privacy, not impenetrability — but at least they would have a warning before someone made it through the gate and up the driveway. She didn't expect anyone to know she and Nico were hiding out here, but they couldn't afford to take anything for granted.

Nico pulled the car to a stop in the courtyard. He leaned forward, his arms on the wheel, and gazed up at the Spanish-style mansion. It didn't look huge from the front, but Angel knew it was an illusion. The house was enormous, with eight bedrooms, a wine cellar, and a gym, among other things. The exterior was faced with ivory stucco, the windows framed with blue shutters, and palm trees provided shade to the interior without totally blocking the sunlight.

"Nice," he said approvingly.

"Thanks," Angel said. She heard the note of sarcasm in her voice and felt like she should explain. "I still don't know how I feel about all of this stuff."

He turned to look at her. "What stuff?"

"All the stuff bought with my father's blood money."

"How do you know the house wasn't built with legitimate income from Rossi Development?"

She thought about it. Everything was all tangled up together. The good and bad, the moral and immoral, the love and hate.

"I guess I don't."

"Maybe that's a blessing," he said, taking her hand.

"Maybe."

They went inside, and Angel opened the windows and the doors leading to the balconies and terraces. The house was just like she remembered it, with soaring ceilings, expansive rooms, and an elaborate iron banister that wound with the curved staircase to the second floor.

When she was done airing out the house, she returned to the ground floor to find Nico standing on the terrace, looking out over the infinity pool and lagoon, and beyond that, to the open ocean in the distance.

"Will this work?" she asked him.

"It will," he said. "Thank you."

She reached up to smooth the crease in his forehead. "What's wrong?"

"I wish you'd go back to New York."

She dropped her arm, stung by his words. "You don't want me here?"

"That's not it." He pulled her into his arms. "Sometimes I think I can't breathe without you."

"Then why?" she asked.

He looked down at her. "I won't be able to live with myself if something happens to you. You know that, right?"

She stretched to kiss him. "Which is why nothing is going to happen to me. We're going to meet Luca, get a handle on what's going on, and decide what to do next. No one even knows we're here, and it's not like anyone would suspect I'm hanging out with my former kidnapper."

A brief flash of misery crossed his features. She wrapped her arms around his neck. "Don't."

"Don't what?" His voice was gruff.

"Don't torture yourself over the past," she said. "Trust me, it doesn't change anything. And I don't think I'd want to change it anyway."

He shook his head. "You can't mean that, Angel. If I hadn't had Luca and Dante kidnap you, your life would be just as it was before."

It was what she'd once wanted. Her old life back. Her old naivety. But that meant not knowing Nico. It meant never feeling the mysterious and powerful connection to the man who was now part of her. Would she wish him away? Wish away what they had? The answer was obvious; she wished her father hadn't died in the flat in London, wished she and David had a chance to talk to him about all the lies he'd told. She wished finding out the truth hadn't been so painful. But to wish anything else would be to undo what had happened between her and Nico, and whatever the future held, she was surprised to realize she didn't want that.

"What I had before was a lie. I'll take the truth." She pressed her body to his. "I'll take this."

She didn't add the rest of it. That she still didn't know if she could live with his connection to the Syndicate, that she didn't know how their lives could possibly blend together after this new crisis passed.

They were interrupted by the buzzing of the intercom, and Angel reluctantly pulled away from Nico to press the button.

"Yes?"

"Angel?" The voice was a little tinny, but she would have recognized it anywhere. "It's Luca. I'm here."

13

"I hope you have something new for me," Nico said.

Luca looked around the high ceilinged kitchen, his gaze continuing to the lagoon beyond the terrace doors. Angel had forgotten how attractive he was — not like Nico, not for her anyway — but still. Luca was tall, with the compact muscle of someone who could quietly and discreetly kick ass. His dark hair was always a little messy over pronounced cheekbones and a strong jaw, and his eyes were a startlingly glacial shade of blue.

"I wish I did," he said, returning his eyes to Nico. "It's like a tomb out there. No one's talking."

"Then I'll go back to New York and make them talk," Nico growled.

Luca shook his head. "Since you left town, the men have been left alone. No more harassment, no more theft. No more data breaches either."

Nico's eyes flashed green. "My staying away isn't a long-term solution."

"I agree," Luca said. "But coming back right now would be counterproductive."

"Well, I'm not staying here," Nico said, pacing to the big window. "The Miami family makes the rest of the Syndicate look hi-tech."

"You could go see Raneiro."

"I asked for his help last time," Nico said without turning around. "I have to take care of this myself."

"London?" Luca suggested. "Farrell helped you with Carlo." He shot an apologetic glance at Angel.

"I'm not hiding." Nico's voice was threaded with steel. "I'll go to LA."

Angel stood straighter. "LA?"

"You said John Lando didn't know anything," Luca said, as if she hadn't spoken.

"No, I said he claimed not to know anything," Nico corrected him. "And I never trust a man's word over the phone. Too easy to lie."

"Will someone please tell me why we'd go to LA?" Angel asked.

"*We* won't go to LA," Nico said. "I will."

She crossed her arms over her chest, resisting the urge to argue. That's what a rational person would do, isn't it? Find out the details? Get all the information before assuming it would be best to go with Nico instead of jumping at the chance for no other reason than that she couldn't stand the thought of being apart from him again?

"What's in LA?" she asked.

"The data breach was routed through some dummy IP addresses in Asia, but it originated in LA," Luca explained. "John Lando runs the Syndicate's operation out there."

She searched her memory. "Isn't John Lando an… actor? Or a director or something?"

"Producer," Luca clarified. "But he's head of the LA family, too. The movie stuff is a front for the Syndicate's business."

"More like the Syndicate is a front for his movie business," Nico said.

"So we would go to LA and do what?" Angel asked.

"*I* would go to LA and talk to John in person," Nico said. "Then I'd have Sara Falco run those words you found in Frank's office and see if she gets a hit that would give me some direction."

"Sounds good," Angel said. "I can help."

"We're not arguing about this," Nico said tightly.

Luca cleared his throat. "Mind if I clean up?"

Angel forced her eyes from Nico. "Come on. I'll show you to one of the rooms."

She led Luca up the curved staircase and left him in a guest room with an en suite bath. Then she went into her old bedroom and moved the few clothes she had stored in the dresser and closet into one of the other rooms. She couldn't stay in a bedroom where her father had kissed her goodnight, couldn't think about her mother's soft hands tucking her in. She still didn't know if her mother had been aware of her father's illegal business activities. She would probably never know, and she was still trying to find a way to live with that.

She took a bath, half hoping Nico would come in and join her. It had only been twelve hours since she'd felt his hands on her naked body, and already she was hungry for him. She'd become a slave to his touch, and she was both disgusted with herself and slightly thrilled by the realization that her body could respond so single-mindedly to someone.

She dried off and slipped on a filmy tank dress of emerald silk. She'd bought it freshman year when she'd come to the beach with friends and had forgotten to pack it when she'd gone back to New York. It was a little shorter than she wore her dresses now, but it was cool and breezy, perfect for the Miami heat. She twisted her hair into a loose chignon and padded on bare feet to the kitchen.

Nico and Luca were on the terrace. They were extraordinarily beautiful with their dark hair, perfectly formed bodies, and easy grace, and she leaned against the doorjamb, listening to them talk in soft murmurs while the sun sunk in the west. She couldn't hear what they were saying, but she waited for what looked like a lull in their conversation to step outside.

"Hey." She ran a hand through Nico's hair as she took the chaise next to him.

He captured her hand, kissed her palm. "Hey."

"What are you two whispering about?"

Nico shot Luca a warning glance.

"Nothing," Nico said.

"Sounds like something a kid says when he's been coloring on the walls," Angel said.

"Well, I'm fresh out of crayons," he said, "so you have nothing to worry about."

"Hmmm…"

"I was going to start dinner," Nico said, "but there's nothing in the fridge."

"I didn't have time to call someone," Angel said. She laughed. "Actually, I'm not even sure who I'd call. I have no idea how to keep all of this stuff running."

"I'll have Jenna set up some property management agreements for you," Nico said. "But not until this is over. I don't want anyone to know you're with me right now."

She knew it was for her own protection, but it still hurt. After all they'd been through, they had to remain a secret. Then again, did she want people to know about her and Nico? Was she ready for what that would mean for her? For David?

"Well, I don't know about you two, but I'm starving," Luca said. "Want me to make a take-out run?"

Nico looked over at her, his eyes lingering on her face before dropping to the short dress pooling around her thighs. "Let's go out."

"Nico…" Angel started.

"No one knows we're here," Nico said. "And we'll avoid the areas where the Syndicate does business. I know my way around. It won't be hard."

Luca rubbed the stubble at his chin. "I don't know…"

Nico stood, pulling Angel up with him. "We're in Miami, probably only for a day or two. Let's go blow off some steam with the tourists."

Luca hesitated, then nodded. Probably because he knew as well as Angel how futile it was to argue with Nico once he'd made up his mind about something.

"So we're going to party, is what you're saying," Angel said.

"We're going to eat," Nico said. "Then we're going to party."

14

They started with classic Cuban sandwiches at a tiny deli near the beach. The pork was so flavorful, the chicken so tender, that Angel groaned when she bit into the crusty bread. They washed the sandwiches down with cold beer, then headed to a nightclub a couple blocks from the water. It was about as far as they could get from the tense, exclusive atmosphere of Farrell Black's club in London, and they did three quick shots of tequila before joining the crush of writhing bodies on the dance floor.

Multi-colored lights flashed over the room, and EDM beat through the speakers posted around the room, the floor shaking to the rhythm of the music. The liquor was working its way into Angel's bloodstream, warming her from the inside out, loosening her inhibitions. She laughed, losing herself to the music and the collective liberation of the people around her.

She lifted her arms over her head and shook her hips until Nico's eyes flashed with desire through the half dark of the room. He tried to grab her, but she didn't want to make Luca feel left out, so she eluded Nico's grasp and danced with them both, the three of them packed together in a position that would have been way too intimate if not for the tequila, the intimacy of their shared experiences, the music and darkness that made it seem like the real world was a million miles away.

The chignon had shaken loose, and sweat was beading between her breasts when Luca waved them off and headed for the bar. He hadn't been gone ten seconds when Nico took her hand and pulled her to him, his hands dropping to her ass as he moved against her. She lifted her arms and wrapped them around his neck, his erection hard against her belly as they moved in time to the beat.

She tipped her head back, lost in the music and the feel of Nico's hands on her body through the thin material of her dress. The crowd pressed all around them, and Nico turned her around, his hips still moving with hers, so her ass was nestled against his hips. His hands slid down to her upper thighs, and she leaned her head back against his shoulder, the two of them still moving to the music.

He dropped his mouth to her collarbone, his tongue leaving a trail of heat all the way to her neck. His cock was more insistent now. The feel of it against her ass sent a flood of warmth to her core, and she didn't protest when his hands moved up the bare skin of her thighs, the dress and the crowd hiding his movements. She gasped as he slid his hands down her belly, slipping them into her panties, but there was no one to hear her. Everyone was as lost as she was in the flashing lights and music and abandon.

His palm cupped the mound of her sex, their hips moving together in time to the music, as the silky material of her dress draped around his wrists. Then his fingers were sliding over her soft folds, setting loose a tidal wave of lust inside her body. She wondered vaguely if anyone could see what he was doing to her, but she couldn't focus long enough to really care. He stroked her clit, swollen with need, and swayed behind her, his cock demanding attention against her ass. She had the insane desire to lift her dress, to feel him penetrate her right on the dance floor, to let him fuck her while everyone moved around them.

A moment later, he thrust two fingers inside of her. She cried out, but no one seemed to notice, and she moved her hips, rocking against his fingers, the flat of his palm stimulating her with every motion of their bodies.

He leaned down, whispering into her ear. "You're wet, Angel."

She was panting now, oblivious to everything but the rhythmic stroke of his fingers as her body barreled toward orgasm.

"Nico," she gasped, turning her head toward his neck as she leaned into him.

"That's right," he murmured in her ear. "You're going to come hard for me right here."

It was an order and a statement of fact. Her body had passed the point of no return. There was nothing but Nico's fingers moving in and out of her, and her mind was overrun with memories of his muscled body dominating hers while he thrust into her.

She was delirious with desire. She wanted him now. In her pussy. In her mouth. Everywhere.

He bit down gently on her earlobe. "I'm going to remind you who owns you tonight, baby. And I'm going to do it by fucking you until you scream."

The words — and the images they brought to mind — sent her over the edge. She let go, and the orgasm washed over her like a waterfall, white light exploding behind her eyelids.

He didn't take his fingers out of her until she stopped shuddering. Then he held her up, swaying with her while she caught her breath. When she stopped trembling, he turned her to face him and lowered his mouth to hers, his tongue igniting a new spark in her belly.

He pulled back to look at her, and the desire in his eyes was so naked she half expected him to take her there. "Let's get out of here."

15

She was drifting through a pleasant unconsciousness when a shrill sound startled her awake. It took her a moment to orient herself. Then she saw her phone shimmying across the bedside table, her brother's name lit up on the screen.

She contemplated letting it go to voice mail. There had been times when she and Nico were apart that she wondered if she'd imagined his hold on her. If she'd magnified the primal connection they shared, the way their bodies worked together like finely tuned instruments. But any doubts she may have had were quickly extinguished the night before. Nico had been true to his word, staking claim to her body long after they'd stumbled home from the club. The sun had been lighting the sky when they finally drifted off to sleep, and it was only a little bit brighter in the room now. They couldn't have been asleep more than an hour.

But David never called this early unless it was important, and she was all too aware of their role as emergency contact for each other. They didn't have anyone else left.

"This better be good," she said after she picked up the phone.

"Ange, it's me. I - "

"I know who it is," she said, laying back on the pillow. Nico, still half asleep, threw an arm around her. "What I don't know is why you're - "

"You have to listen, Ange!"

She sat up as the fear in his voice became obvious. "What's going on? Are you okay?"

"I'm okay, but - "

Another voice, cold and familiar, came on the line. "I wouldn't take that to the bank if I were you."

It took her a few seconds to get the name out of her mouth. "Dante?"

Nico sat up like a shot next to her, throwing his feet over the bed and onto the floor.

"The one and only," Dante said.

"What are you doing with my brother?"

Nico held out his hand for the phone. She shook her head, the icy grip of dread slowly closing around her heart.

"We just met," Dante said. "We're still getting acquainted. Where we go from here is up to you."

"What do you want?"

"I want what's owed to me," he said, his voice low.

She shook her head, like that would help her understand his demand, or better yet, prove the whole thing a nightmare. "Money?"

"Do you really think money solves everything, bitch?"

She glanced at Nico, and the look of sheer rage on his face scared her almost as much as the fact that Dante had her brother.

"Just tell me what you want," she said, trying to keep her voice even. Desperation was a losing strategy with someone like Dante.

"I want New York," he said. "All of it."

"New York?" she searched her mind, trying to decipher the meaning behind his demand.

"The New York territory," he said. "It was supposed to go to my father. Which means it was supposed to go to me. And you can bet that if we were in charge, things would be a whole lot different."

"I don't have any control over that," she said, hope lighting like a tiny ember inside her. If she could make him understand that she didn't have the power to give him what he wanted, maybe he would let David go.

"No, but you have control over the motherfucker who does."

"Nico?"

Nico closed his hand around her phone, trying to get it from her. She slapped his hand away and stood, walking to the window.

"Bingo," Dante said. "And I suggest you do whatever is necessary to make him forfeit the territory."

"I don't... I don't even know how this works," she said, unable to keep the desperation out of her voice. "Isn't that something that goes through Raneiro Donati?"

She waited for his response. Instead she heard a wet slap, followed by a thud and a groan that she knew instinctively was David.

"Don't hurt him!" she cried, then immediately regretted the show of weakness. "I'll… I'll talk to Nico, but I think you're overestimating my influence."

His laugh was a mean and bitter bark. "I highly doubt that. In fact, I'd be willing to bet he'd do just about anything for your tight little cunt."

She took a deep breath, glad Nico was still on the bed where he couldn't hear the way Dante was talking to her.

"I'll do my best. Just please… don't hurt my brother. He's not part of this at all."

"Correction," Dante said. "He wasn't part of this. Now he is, and you're going to have him back in pieces if you don't find a way to get me what I want."

"How do I contact you?" She couldn't see through her fear. She needed to get off the phone, talk to Nico, figure out what to do next.

"You don't," he said. "I'll be in touch in seventy-two hours. And I hope for the sake of this pansy-ass that you've got good news for me."

The fact that an animal like Dante had her gentle brother made her want to scream. But his insult to David made her want to weep. He'd been so hurt when their father hadn't been able to accept that he'd been gay. Dante was a reflection of the hatred that made David a target for people who weren't fit to breathe the same air.

She swallowed her anger. "Do I have your word you won't hurt him until then?"

He laughed. "You don't have shit."

The line went dead.

16

"The call came from LA," Luca said, putting his phone down.

"Is Sara sure?" Nico asked.

"She's sure," Luca said, running a hand through his messy hair. "She was able to trace it to LA before the signal went dead. Thank god for Dante's giant ego. The dumbass probably used David's phone as some kind of mind fuck to Angel. He would have been better off with a throwaway."

Nico walked to the edge of the terrace and looked out over the water. He wanted to go to Angel, curled up on a chaise, looking like death, but he didn't trust himself. Wasn't sure he could see the fear in her eyes without setting fire to anyone who had ever known Dante, to John Lando and his family in LA, to anything and everyone who might have something to do with the emptiness in Angel's eyes.

Coward, a voice whispered in his head.

As much as he wanted to deny it, he knew it was the truth. He could take on the most violent of criminals, could ruin them financially, kill them with his bare hands. But he feared seeing blame in Angel's eyes and knowing it belonged to him. She had been safe, dammit. She'd escaped the clutches of her father's life. Of Nico's life.

She'd come back to it all to help him.

He half considered giving in to Dante's demands. Fuck, let him have the New York territory. Nico almost didn't care anymore.

Then he thought of his parents — murdered in cold blood at the hands of Dante and Carlo Rossi — and all the people who worked for him. He had promised them a new vision for the family, one that was sustainable for the twenty-first century. Maybe even one they could live with. It was clear now that Dante was behind the attacks against them. He couldn't cut and run. Not even for Angel.

And there was something else; he knew now that Angel wouldn't be safe until Dante was dead. Nico wouldn't make the same mistake he'd made in London by letting Dante out alive. Not this time.

"So we go to LA," Angel said from the chaise, her voice flat. "Just like we planned."

Nico turned to look at her. "That was never the plan, Angel," he said. "The plan was for me to go to LA, and that's still the plan."

"He's my brother," she said softly.

Nico took a deep breath. "I know that. And that's why I'm going to go get him for you."

"He's *my* brother!" she shouted, like he hadn't heard her the first time. Her voice echoed off the stone terrace, and she stood, crossing to stand in front of him. She looked him in the eyes. "You can't ask me to stay behind, Nico." She sucked in a shuddery breath. "You just can't."

He wanted to say yes, to let her come with him simply because she asked. But he'd spent six months without her. Six months during which he sometimes wondered if he'd even wake up the next morning, if the pain of being without her would kill him silently in his sleep, like a long illness coming to an end in the dead of night. She was the only thing in his life that mattered, and he wasn't willing to lose her again. Not to Dante, and not to all the things that could go wrong while Nico went after him to get David back.

"I can and I will," Nico said firmly. "You'll go to Maine and wait while I get David."

She crossed her arms over her chest, and he didn't know whether to be relieved or scared by the familiar gesture. It meant she still had some fight in her. And that could be good and bad.

"I'm going to LA," she said. "With or without you. I'm Carlo Rossi's daughter. I'm sure I can get my own meeting with John Lando."

"Goddammit, Angel!" She jumped a little as he shouted, his frustration bubbling over. "Did you forget what happened when you refused to stay at the flat in London?"

Her eyes flashed. "I did not."

"Then why can't you trust me on this one?" he asked.

"Because this is my brother's life," she said. "He's my responsibility, and it's my fault he's mixed up in all of this."

Her words made him hesitate. He'd been too quick to assume she would blame him. He hadn't thought about the possibility that she would feel guilty about the fact that David was in danger. That she would blame herself.

"This isn't your fault," Nico said, putting his hands on her shoulders, looking into her eyes.

"I wanted to help you," she said. And then, more softly. "I wanted to see you."

He pulled her into his arms. "I know. But I'm not letting you take the blame for the actions of an animal like Dante."

"For all we know," Luca said from the other side of the terrace, "Dante would have come after you or David anyway. This isn't necessarily tied to the fact that you tried to help Nico. You didn't exactly make your location a secret the past six months, and I think it's safe to say Dante is behind Carmine's death, and everything else that has happened."

She pulled away from Nico. "It doesn't matter whose fault it is," she said. "I need to be there when you get David out, and I need to be as close to him as I can until then."

Nico rubbed his forehead, sensing his position slipping away. Angel took advantage of the opening to continue.

"I'm in this now, whether you want me to be or not, whether I want to be or not. And this only proves that hiding isn't any kind of protection."

He exhaled his frustration. She was right, and the rational side of his mind — the side whose number one goal wasn't to hide Angel from anything that could so much as give her a hangnail — knew it.

"Fine," he said. "But you let me take the lead with John Lando, and anyone else in the west coast family. We don't know where their loyalties lay. Until we do, we have to assume it's not with us."

She nodded, but she didn't look any happier about the victory than he felt. He turned to Luca.

"Who do we have out there that we can trust?"

Luca rubbed the stubble on his chin. He hadn't been in his room when Nico went to get him after Dante's call. Nico had called his cell, and Luca had shown up rumpled and tired twenty minutes later. Must have gotten lucky with the spring break crowd.

"Ivan Russo? He left last year. But not because he didn't believe in what you were doing. I think he had a girl out west."

Nico shook his head. "I don't want anyone associated with the Syndicate. Too risky right now."

Luca looked surprised. "You think this goes deeper than Dante?"

"I don't know," Nico said. "But I don't think we should take for granted that it doesn't."

"What about Locke Montgomery?" Luca suggested.

Nico thought about it. Locke was a contradiction in terms; an independently wealthy ex-Black Ops soldier who now ran top secret commando missions all over the world — always his way, and only when he thought the end justified the means. He was also a botanist who believed strongly in the power of medicinal marijuana, and his growth operation was responsible for millions in tax revenue to the State of California - and for easing the pain of people who still lived in states where it was illegal.

Nico had learned about Locke when he first started reorganizing the family. He'd met with heavy — and violent — resistance and had needed help taking down a group of persistent dissenters. Locke came highly recommended, and Nico had liked that the man had no long-standing loyalties to any of the families or to the Syndicate at large. He had only agreed to help squash the uprising after reading Nico's business plan, and Nico had been surprised to realize it wasn't the additional revenue that appealed to Locke — it was the prospect of a more enlightened approach to the traditions of organized crime.

Nico was good at reading people, but he'd never been as baffled as the day he'd met Locke Montgomery. Part of him wanted to draw his weapon in response to the undercurrent of violence lurking below Locke's surface. The other part had wanted to kick off his shoes and smoke a joint with him.

And Nico didn't smoke.

"That's an interesting possibility," Nico said.

"He's loyal to decency, not people or ideology. I think he would get behind offering you safe harbor if it was to save Angel's brother."

"David," Angel said softly. "His name's David."

Luca nodded. "David."

"I'll call Locke now," Nico said. He turned to Angel as he headed inside. "Pack your bags."

17

Angel arrived in Los Angeles later that day with her heart in her throat. She felt better knowing David was close, but not knowing what was happening to him was killing her. She'd fought panic almost every moment since Dante's call, finding solace only in the numbness that sometimes settled over her like a gift.

Nico opened the door of the car Luca had arranged for them, and Angel slid into the backseat. There were no friendly greetings with the driver this time, no kiss on the cheek as with their driver in Rome last fall. They were off the grid as far as the Syndicate was concerned, laying low and keeping their movements a secret from everyone but Luca, who had gone back to New York to check on the business.

She leaned her head on Nico's shoulder as they headed south. She knew he blamed himself for what had happened to David, but she wasn't letting herself off the hook so easily. She should have known better than to step back into her father's world. Into Nico's world. She'd barely escaped with her life last time. She'd been naive to think that she could dip her toe in the water without being sucked back in. And while naivety wasn't a crime, in this case, selfishness was. Going to Nico had been nothing but selfish. Now she could only hope to save David's life and put as much distance between them and the Syndicate as possible. They would sell their father's business, officially hand over the Syndicate's operations to Frank. Then they would go somewhere far away.

A vise closed around her heart. It would mean leaving Nico behind. She couldn't have it all; her brother, their safety, Nico. But she wouldn't think about that now.

They sat on the freeway for over two hours, moving at a crawl in the infamous LA traffic, then broke free just after San Diego. The sun was setting, lighting the Pacific on fire as it sunk toward the horizon, when they finally turned onto a winding road leading up a hill of scraggy brush bordered with palm trees.

The house was Spanish in style, with a white stucco facade and a red tile roof. It was set on a cliff high above the water, and Angel could just make out a meandering path to the private cove below.

The driver pulled into a gravel courtyard and they got out, retrieved their bags, and headed for the front door. Nico rang the bell, and they glanced at each other as it echoed on the other side of the door.

A minute later it was opened by a tall, muscled man in jeans. He looked at them from eyes that were so dark, it took her a minute to realize they were blue. His sculpted chest was tan, bare except for some kind of pendant tied with rope around his neck and a strange tattoo that covered his shoulders and continued onto his back. He had thick, wavy blond hair, the antithesis of the carefully maintained style worn by Nico and every man she'd ever met who was part of the Syndicate.

She was simultaneously intrigued and afraid. Then a smile broke out across the man's face, and he reached out a hand to Nico.

"You made it."

Nico nodded. "We did." They shook hands, and Nico turned to Angel. "Angel, this is Locke Montgomery. Locke, Angel."

She wondered if he'd omitted her last name on purpose. "Hello," she said, shaking his hand. "Thank you for letting us stay."

"It sounds like you need a friend," Locke said. "And I try to be a friend when circumstances allow."

They followed him down a long tile hall. Angel tried to make out the design tattooed onto his back, but it looked abstract, and she finally gave up. They emerged into an expansive room furnished with patterned rugs, overstuffed couches, and rustic tables and overlooking the ocean. The glass doors opened around a two-sided fireplace split between the living room and a deck that seemed to hover over the cliffs above the sea. A homey but elaborate kitchen beckoned from the other end of the room.

"Nice place," Nico said, looking around.

"It's private, and that's what I need. Sounds like what you need, too."

Nico nodded. "It is."

"There's a security system attached to the property and the house. I'll show you how to work it before I leave tomorrow."

"Not because of us, I hope," Angel said.

Locke flashed her a devastating grin, and she suddenly felt sorry for any woman he turned it on. Was resisting even an option?

"Not a chance," he said. "I have a job to attend to. But you're welcome to stay as long as you like."

He showed them to a large bedroom overlooking the water. An enormous canopy bed, draped with sheer white curtains and facing a private balcony, dominated the space. The early morning call from Dante together with the news about David and the long flight to LA had caught up with her. She wanted nothing more than to crawl under the covers and sleep to the sound of the waves rushing the shore below. But Locke wanted to show them around, and she reluctantly left the room behind.

The house was surprisingly big, shaped like an "L" around a central courtyard planted with red bougainvillea and fragrant jasmine. She thought she spotted lemon trees, and maybe even avocado. She wondered how many gardeners it took to maintain such a large piece of land, unusual for Southern California where the lots tended to be small and crowded.

They continued to the pool area off the living room. At first she thought it had been left to grow naturally, but when she looked closer she could see order under the chaos, could see the careful design that made the pool area blend into the surrounding landscape, scrubby and mountainous and not at all what most people imagined when they pictured California. It was like happening upon an oasis in the middle of the desert.

There was a greenhouse at the back of the property — used to test new strains, Locke said, whatever that meant — and the winding path she'd spotted earlier that led to the private beach below the house. She couldn't help wondering what Locke did for a living. He was young, probably Nico's age, and the place must have cost a fortune.

The sun had set by the time they were done. Locke threw three thick steaks on a grill outside, and Angel threw together a salad with contents from Locke's fridge. He put on music, and they ate on the patio, putting down two bottles of wine between them. Nico filled Locke in on the details of David's kidnapping, and Angel felt the bottom fall out of her stomach all over again. She was here, in this beautiful place eating this beautiful food, while her brother was scared and imprisoned somewhere in the same state.

She pushed her plate away and took another drink of her wine.

It was late by the time they finished. Locke waved off their offers of help cleaning up, and she and Nico headed to their bedroom at the other end of the house. She could hardly keep her eyes open as he led her to the bed. She sat on the edge of the cushy mattress while he opened the glass door leading to the deck, and a wash of sea air drifted into the room with the sound of the tide rolling in below.

He crossed the room and knelt at her feet, then gently removed her shoes. "Want to shower before bed?"

She shook her head, feeling like a child. "I'm too tired."

He unbuttoned her jeans, and she lifted her hips so he could slide them off. Then he lifted the T-shirt over her head so she was sitting in her bra and panties. He reached for her feet.

"Lay down, baby." He swung her legs onto the bed, and she slipped them under the covers.

"Aren't you coming to bed?" she asked as he tucked her in.

"Of course," he said, kissing her forehead. "I'll be there before you know it."

She closed her eyes and let the warmth of his protection wash over her. She wouldn't have it forever. But she had it now.

18

She woke to the sound of the ocean, and she lay in bed for a long time, wondering if David could hear it, too. If Nico and Luca were right, they were on the same side of the country, at least.

It was cold comfort. Already twenty-four hours had passed. They had two more days to find something that would lead them to her brother before Dante called again. The thought threatened to make her crazy, and she got up and threw on a sundress before padding down to the kitchen on bare feet. She could see Nico and Locke talking on the patio, but there was coffee, so she poured herself a cup before joining them.

"Good morning," she said, lowering herself into the chair next to Nico.

"Morning," Locke said. "Sleep okay?"

She nodded, feeling a little guilty. She didn't think she'd be able to sleep knowing David was in danger, but her whole body had started shutting down the minute she hit the luxurious bed. She had a vague memory of Nico's sliding in next to her, of nestling in the crook of his arm just to be sure he was really there, but that was where her recollection of the night ended.

Nico took her hand. "You needed it. You're not good to anyone dead on your feet."

As if he knew exactly what she'd been thinking. As if he knew how hard it was to eat or drink or breathe — to feel anything good — knowing David was under Dante's control.

She took a sip of her coffee and looked out over the water. It was late April, and there was a thick layer of cloud cover overhead. No California sunshine for them.

Nico stood. "I'm heading out for my meeting with John."

"I'll come with you," Angel said, setting her coffee cup down.

He put a gentle hand on her shoulder. "You should stay. He won't speak as freely if you're there. And Luca's supposed to be getting back to us with the results of the search on the words you found in your father's office. I told him to call you."

"You did?" Other than Boston, it was the first time he'd trusted her with a piece of their strategy.

"Of course, I did." He bent to kiss her head. "I'll be back this afternoon."

He disappeared into the house, and a few minutes later, she heard the sound of a powerful engine starting up in the courtyard. She looked over at Locke with a raised eyebrow.

"Porsche," he said.

"Of course."

She'd stopped being surprised by the level of raw testosterone surrounding Nico. It must be in the water or something; all the men he knew were controlling and possessive. They liked fast cars. They made no apologies for enjoying the power they wielded, even when they wielded that power judiciously. A year ago, a man like that would have been a turnoff. A douchebag, according to the other girls at school.

Now she found that they weren't as one-dimensional as she would have expected. There was something elemental about them — their desire to protect, to win, to dominate. And maybe there was something primitive about the fact that it turned her on, too. Maybe there was something buried in the psychology of the species, something that couldn't let go of the survival instinct that had forced man to protect his tribe and had made women seek out that protection.

Did that make her some kind of simpering idiot? A throwback to a time when women were consigned to the kitchen and the bedroom? She didn't think so. She still wanted things for herself. Still valued her intellect and her ability to contribute.

But damn. She kind of liked these alpha males.

"I have to leave in a bit," Locke said. "But first I'm going to catch some waves. Want to come down to the beach?"

"Can I get cell service down there?" She didn't want to miss Luca's call.

"You can," he said.

"Okay."

She changed into her bathing suit, glad she'd thought to bring it, and met Locke in the living room. He looked like a bronze god, his muscled torso exposed over an unzipped wetsuit that hung around his lean hips, a very pronounced "V" pointing downward. She couldn't think about any man but Nico with lust, but if she'd been able to, Locke would probably do the trick.

They exited through the patio doors and past an open-air shower at the top of the hill. He grabbed a surfboard leaning against the wood that held the shower head and started down the winding pathway.

The ocean was churning gray under the overcast sky, but the air was warm, the breeze gentle. It felt wrong to see the beauty in it when she didn't know what was happening to David. She was thinking about turning around, waiting for Luca's call in the house, when Locke spoke.

"Coastal eddy," Locke said.

"Excuse me?"

"The clouds." He tipped his head to the sky. "Everyone thinks it's always sunny in Southern California, but the coastal eddy creates a marine layer that lasts through June. Sometimes into July."

"I didn't know that," she said. "Although I don't mind it. I'm definitely an east coast girl."

"Well, east coast girls are hip, I hear."

She smiled at his Beach Boys reference.

"Yeah, but California girls…"

"… are pretty hot, too," he said.

She kept walking with him to the bottom of the hill. Staying inside wouldn't do anything to help David. She would only stare at the clock, count the minutes left to help him. He wouldn't want her to punish herself that way.

The cove was private, marked at either end by high, craggy cliffs that blocked off the property from surrounding homes and centered by a perfect strip of sand.

"How long have you had this place?" Angel asked, laying down the beach towel Locke had handed her on their way out.

He started pulling up his wetsuit. "About four years."

She tried to hide her surprise. He already looked so young. How had he been able to afford such a place in a real estate market that commanded millions for even the smallest patches of beach front property?

"It's really beautiful," she said. "I'm surprised you leave at all. I'm not sure I could."

"I'm more or less at home anywhere," he said, zipping the wetsuit. "But this place does have a special kind of energy, doesn't it?"

"It does."

He picked up his board. "Catch you on the flip side."

She sat on her towel, tucking her phone into one of the corners, and watched him sprint down the beach. She loved Nico. Wanted him like no other. But she wasn't dead yet.

Leaning back on her elbows, she watched Locke paddle out to deeper waters. He moved effortlessly, catching the waves at just the right moment, maneuvering the board like it was an extension of his body. He looked so free, and for a moment, she had the desire to join him, to coast above the water until the wave deposited her into its depths. Maybe she would learn to surf when this was all over. Maybe David would learn with her. Why not?

After a while she walked down to the water, careful to stay out of Locke's way. She dove under a big wave and emerged on the other side of it invigorated and refreshed. She'd forgotten how much she enjoyed the ocean, how freeing it was to swim and float, letting it carry her like a leaf drifting down a mountain stream. She stayed out for a long time, riding over some of the waves, feeling her stomach lift as they carried her over the sandy ocean bottom, and diving under others, the muffled crash of them breaking overhead.

Locke was already back on the beach when she finally came in.

"Not a sun worshipper, I take it?" he asked as she dried off.

She shook her head. "Not really. It's kind of boring."

He laughed appreciatively. "I couldn't agree more."

They made their way up the path, and Angel headed to her room to take a shower. She was drying off when her cell phone rang from the bathroom counter. Luca's name was displayed on the screen. She picked it up.

"Luca?"

"Angel," he said. "How's it going?"

"You tell me." She didn't want to waste words on small talk.

"Sara ran some searches on "Strand" and "South Bay"."

"And?" she said, walking naked into the bedroom. "Did she find anything?"

"Yes and no."

Angel sighed. "Can you be more specific?"

"They're common words," Luca said. "Between searches run separately and together, she came up with school, neighborhoods, even retirement homes, from Southern California to Florida to Portugal."

"Southern California?"

"Don't get your hopes up, Angel," Luca warned.

"But if the call came from LA and the piece of paper from my father's office had words leading to LA - "

"Leading to lots of places," Luca reminded her.

Angel slipped a bra on around the phone. "Seems like quite a coincidence."

"I agree, and you can feel free to start with the hits there. I just don't want you to miss something else that might be important because you've already convinced yourself the words are connected to LA."

"What exactly am I looking for?" she asked, pulling on a skirt.

"I'm going to send you a list of all the hits Sara got. We need you to go through it and tell us if anything jumps out at you; a name, a location, anything that could be connected to you or David."

"The words might not be connected to us at all," Angel said. "And I have no way to know if they're connected to Dante, to where he's holding David."

Luca sighed. "I'm not going to lie; it's a long shot. But it's all we've got right now. And Sara's going to go over the search results with a fine-tooth comb, cross-referencing them with everything we know about Dante, his history, his family."

"Okay," she said. "I'll do my best."

"Good. I'm sending them to Locke's computer now. His servers are encrypted. Just ask him to sign you in."

"Thanks, Luca."

"You're welcome." He hesitated. "How are you holding up?"

"I don't know," she said. "It seems a little surreal, which is probably the only reason I'm not losing it right now."

"Shock is a survival mechanism. Use the distance it gives you to work on finding something that leads to David."

"I will."

"Talk soon."

The line went dead, and Angel dropped onto the bed in her skirt and bra. Her reliable numbness faded into the background long enough to allow for panic. Luca was trying to stay positive, trying to keep her positive. But they all knew the truth, even if it was unspoken; if finding David was dependent on connecting three commonly used words to a man she didn't know, they were screwed.

19

Nico sat in the lobby of Lando Productions for a full twenty minutes before the
receptionist — a leggy brunette - showed him into John's office. He had no way of
knowing if it was intentional discourtesy or just more of John's obliviousness about
family protocol, so he took deep breaths while he followed the brunette to an office at the
end of a long, carpeted hall.

Angel needed John. And that meant Nico would do whatever it took to get what
they could from him.

The receptionist opened the door with a smile, then waited until Nico walked
through it to close it with a quiet click.

John stood behind a modern desk, the streets of Hollywood humming on the other
side of the giant window behind him.

"Nico!" he said, coming around the desk with a smile. "So nice to see you."

"It's been a long time," Nico said as they embraced.

John patted his shoulder. "It has." He gestured to the two upholstered chairs in
front of the desk. "Please, sit."

John Lando was a small man with a soft face and eyes the color of sand. Everything
about him was unremarkable, and Nico marveled again that John somehow found himself
head of the LA family. It's true what people said; it really wasn't what you know, but
whom.

Nico took a seat and looked around the room as John made his way back behind his
desk. It was more generic than Nico would have expected, with gray carpet and furniture
that was obviously expensive but far from inspiring. Framed movie posters provided the
only color in the room, and Nico thought he recognized images from John's last two
films.

"So what can I help you with, Nico?" John asked when he was settled.

"I'm looking for Dante Santoro." Nico had decided to take the direct approach. He had no idea if John was helping Dante in LA, but being direct might throw him off balance enough for Nico to determine if he was hiding something.

"Dante?" John blinked at him.

Nico nodded. "He's off reservation, has taken a hostage. I need to find him."

John opened the top drawer of his desk, fidgeted with something inside before closing it and returning his gaze to Nico. "Well, Nico, I'm not really in the know on this kind of thing."

"I understand," Nico said. "But the last call from Dante came from LA. I figured if anyone knew anything, it would be you."

He wasn't trying to flatter John Lando. The man couldn't care less about being respected outside of the movie industry. Nico was simply hoping to gauge John's reaction, see if he closed up or distanced himself rather than offering to help.

"You give me too much credit," John said. "My time is almost exclusively occupied by my production company. The truth is, Gino Torelli handles most of the family business, an arrangement that works perfectly for me."

He wasn't lying. Gino was John's Underboss, and rumor had it he handled day-to-day family business so John could focus on his movies. It was a weakness with no real consequence; in LA, the movie business reigned supreme. John wielded far more influence as a film executive than he would as Boss of the LA family. It was probably one of the reasons Dante came out west to stage his coup. The U.S. arm of the Syndicate had been headquartered on the east coast since the late 1800s. A takeover would have met with more resistance there, and Dante may have found help harder to find.

"That may be true," Nico said. "But we both know big decisions always go through the man in charge. And that would be you."

He held John's gaze until he broke eye contact, shuffling things nervously around on his desk.

"I'm sorry I can't help. I haven't heard anything about Dante being in LA." He looked up, his eyes unnaturally bright. He might be the worst liar Nico had ever seen. "But I'm having a little party tomorrow night to celebrate funding on a new project. I don't usually mix family business with movie business, but you should come."

It was a fatal mistake on John's part. In an effort to deflect Nico's questions about Dante, John had opened a door he probably didn't want open. And while attending a Hollywood party filled with self-important celebrities was the very last thing Nico wanted to do, it would gain him access to John's house.

"I'd love to come," Nico said.

John's face fell a little. "Great, great."

He scrawled something on a piece of paper and handed it to Nico. "Starts at nine. Ends whenever. And if you end up not being able to make it, I understand."

Nice try, Nico thought.

"I'll be there," he said, standing.

John reached across the desk to his hand. "Looking forward to it."

"I'll just see myself out," Nico said.

He strode to the door and headed down the hall before John could protest, passing the brunette without a word. He was still fuming over the interaction when he hit the street outside. He didn't know if John was actually helping Dante, but the bastard knew something. And Nico had no doubt that John's decision to keep quiet had nothing to do with loyalty and everything to do with cowardice.

There were only two possibilities; either John had made the decision to lay down while Dante defied the rules of the Syndicate, or Gino had made the decision and John had gone along with it. Either way, the man wasn't fit to run the LA family — or any family.

He walked toward Locke's Porsche, parked at the curb. It was as unsatisfying an outcome as he could have imagined. He couldn't rule John out, but he didn't have a solid lead on his involvement either.

What would he tell Angel?

He thought about how she'd looked the night before, eyes wary and sad when he'd tucked her into bed, and felt a fresh burst of admiration for her. She had the heart of a lion. She would fight to get her brother back alive, and he would fight with her. He would burn down the whole city if necessary.

He looked in the rearview mirror, waiting a full minute before a break in traffic allowed him to pull away from the curb.

Fuck, he hated LA.

20

Angel sat back in the dining room chair and rubbed her eyes. Locke had given her the permissions for his server before he'd left, and she'd gone to work the minute the reports from Luca came through via email.

But any hope she'd started with was gone after hours pouring over an endless list of names, places, companies, schools. At first she'd been careful, taking time to really process every hit. That level of detail hadn't lasted long. There was simply too much information, and none of it struck a bell as something that might lead to David. Not that she was anywhere near finished.

She looked at the page on the computer screen; 37 of 362.

Fighting the urge to scream into the empty room, she pushed back from the table and poured a glass of wine from the bottle she'd opened at lunch. Apparently, Locke wasn't only a surfer-slash-commando-slash-entrepreneur-slash-greenthumb; he was also an expert on wines. He'd shown her the wine cellar before he left and had even chosen a lovely Riesling to get her started.

She took a drink of the cold, sweet liquid and closed her eyes, forcing herself to breathe deeply, empty her mind. She wouldn't be able to help David if she couldn't think clearly.

Her thoughts were interrupted by the sound of an engine growing steadily louder as it approached the courtyard. A minute later, the front door opened, and she heard Nico's footsteps in the hall.

"Hey," he said, rounding the corner into the kitchen. His white shirt was open at the neck, revealing a sliver of smooth skin, and his tailored chinos seemed to hug every muscle in his big thighs. He'd been gone all day, but he looked as crisp and fresh as he had this morning. "How was your day?"

She tried to smile, or at least not to look like she wanted to scream. "It was okay. I started on the reports from Luca."

"Yeah?" He took a drink from her glass, then lowered his mouth to hers, sliding his tongue, cold from the wine, over hers until she shivered with anticipation. She knew what his tongue would feel like if he took her nipple in his mouth. Knew how delicious his cold mouth would be sucking her clit. He pulled back to look at her, his eyes a little glassy. "Any luck?"

She forced her thoughts away from Nico's mouth on her body. "Not yet. There's a lot."

He walked over to the table and looked at the open laptop Locke had given her. "Is this it?"

She nodded. "I've been working all day."

"Like a needle in a haystack," he muttered, scrolling over the pages.

"Exactly." His words caused a fresh surge of frustration to roll through her body. "And it might not work at all."

He crossed the room and stopped in front of her, slid his hands into the hair at the back of her head. "Hey," he said softly, "we're going to figure this out."

She pulled away and took a gulp of the wine. "What if we don't?"

"We will," he insisted.

"Maybe we should have a Plan B," she said. "Just in case."

He narrowed his eyes. "What kind of Plan B?"

She swallowed hard, knowing he wouldn't like what she said next. "Well, Dante wants the New York territory, right?"

Nico shook his head. "You can't be serious."

"I'm not saying you should give it to him," she said quickly. She would never ask that of Nico. Would never even want him to do it. The thought of all that power in the hands of someone like Dante — all those people willing to do his bidding — made her sick. "I was just thinking…. maybe there's a way we could get him to think you were giving him the business. Just for show, until he releases David."

"That would never work," he said.

"Why?"

"Because I'd have to make some kind of announcement to make it believable, and you can't come back from something like that." His voice had risen, and she could see from the set of his jaw that he was angry. "You can't tell men like the ones who work for me that they work for someone else and then say 'just kidding' afterward."

"Don't patronize me," Angel snapped. She took a deep breath. "I'm just saying, maybe there's a way to fake it to get David back."

He met her gaze. "I think you're oversimplifying things."

She wanted to rail against him. To tell him it *was* simple; she need to get her brother back unharmed. Nothing else mattered. But even as she thought it, she knew it was a lie. Even a tiny amount of power in the hands of someone like Dante could be catastrophic for a lot of innocent people. She couldn't just blow that off, pretend it didn't matter.

"I know it's not simple," she said. "I just don't like relying on three-hundred-and-sixty-two pages of random words and phrases to find my brother."

He pulled her into his arms, and she let herself sink into his chest, to believe for just a minute that he could make everything right.

"I'm working some other angles," he said, kissing the top of her head.

She looked up at him. "Like what? Did John know anything?"

"He knows something all right," Nico said drily. "He just wouldn't cop to it."

"What do you mean?"

"He claimed not to know anything about Dante being in LA. The problem is, he's not only a coward, he's a terrible liar."

"How do we prove that though?" she asked.

"We attend a party."

"A party?"

"A Hollywood party," he said. "John was so busy trying to move me past the subject of Dante that he invited us to his house."

She pulled away from Nico and paced the floor. "And you're thinking we dig around a little while we're there?"

"They'll probably be watching me," Nico said. "I was thinking you could do it while I keep them busy."

"Won't he make sure his house is clean since you're coming?"

"He'll try," Nico said. "But he'd have to wipe computers, empty drawers, scour every surface for incriminating evidence."

"How do you know he won't?"

Nico laughed a little. "I don't think he's that smart. Not about this anyway. He might be able to make a great movie, but the west coast family is more or less run by his Underboss."

There were a hundred things wrong with the plan. What if she was caught? What if John's Underboss took it upon himself to make sure the place was clean after he found out Nico was coming?

She turned to Nico, not bothering to hide her suspicion. "Why are you letting me do this?"

"What do you mean?" he asked, a little too innocently.

She folded her arms over her chest. "You've gone from wanting to roll me in bubble wrap to letting me dig through John Lando's house during a party? Come on. What's up?"

He sighed. "Look, I'm not about to leave you alone here, two hours from LA, while I go to this party. Which means you're coming with me. And I'm not going to leave you exposed to John's men while I search his house. It's safer for you if I keep their eyes on me. That means you're the one to search John's house."

"So basically, you'll be in more danger than me?"

"Exactly," he said. "Because I'm going to keep my eye on every single one of John's men to make sure you're in the clear."

"Great," she said.

It made sense, and she was confident that John's men wouldn't be a danger to her with Nico watching them. But she wasn't crazy about Nico being in the line of fire either.

"It's the only way," he said. "Unless you want to rely on those three-hundred-and-sixty-two pages of data from Sara."

She sighed. "I don't. Although I'm not giving up on that either."

"We'll cover all our bases," he said, slipping a hand into her shirt and cupping her breast.

"It looks like you're the one covering all your bases," she said.

His chuckle was deep, laced with sex. "On the contrary; I'm trying to cover all your bases."

She swatted at him, but already her pulse had quickened, and she felt her body calling for him. "Now you're just getting cheesy."

He bent his head, flicking his tongue against her neck, moving up to nibble her ear until her breath came fast and shallow.

"Come on," he said. "Let's go for a swim."

"Let me get my bathing suit."

He pulled her toward the sound of the ocean rushing onto the beach. "You won't be needing your bathing suit, Angel."

21

They were having breakfast on the patio the next morning when the intercom sounded at the front gate. Angel flinched, her mind turning to Dante, wondering if he'd sent someone after them. She wasn't worried for herself. But David was out there, counting on her to find him in the next twenty-four hours. And Nico... well, maybe he wasn't what some people would call a good man. But he was her man. And she would rather die than see something happen to him.

He put a gentle hand over hers. "It's nothing. I'm expecting a package."

He went inside and pressed a button on the intercom attached to the security camera. On the display, Angel could just make out a FedEx truck sitting outside the gates.

"Leave it," Nico said into the intercom.

He watched as the driver stepped out of the truck and leaned something against the gate. When he'd left, Nico opened a drawer in the kitchen and removed a revolver.

Angel stood. "Nico?"

"It's just a precaution," he said. "Everything's fine. I'll be right back."

She walked into the house and watched on the camera as he made his way down the drive. Sure enough, he pressed the code to open the gate, retrieved the package, and re-entered Locke's compound without incident. She exhaled loudly, holding a hand to her chest like that would stop the too-fast beating of her heart.

He returned to the house a couple of minutes later, carrying a large brown box.

"What is it?" she asked.

He came toward her and set it on the table. "Open it."

"It's for me?"

"It is."

She went to the kitchen for a knife, then used it to cut the tape at the sides and along the center. Inside the box were two more boxes; one large and white, the other a shoe box.

She looked at him. "What did you do?"

"Open it."

She started with the white box, tied with a silky midnight blue bow. When she lifted the lid, she peeled back several layers of tissue paper before she came to the French blue silk. The fabric was just a whisper as she lifted it out of the box to reveal a filmy floor length dress. The color started as gray-blue at the shoulders, slowly lightening to pale aqua at the hem in a kind of ombre. It had long sleeves, might even have been conservative except for the deep "V" cut into the neckline. A glimpse at the label told her it was Elie Saab.

"It's gorgeous," she said. "But why are you shopping for me? I brought clothes from the house in Miami."

He pulled her into his arms, crushing the dress between them. The silk was a sensual counterpoint to the hard line of his body, and she felt the stirrings of desire as she imagined his hands sliding up her bare legs under the dress.

"Those are Miami clothes," he said. "You needed LA clothes."

She smiled, touched that he was always thinking of her, even when a monster like Dante was after his business, was after him. "I did, huh?"

He nodded, his eyes hooded. "There are shoes, too."

"A dress and shoes?" she asked, trying to be playful in spite of the ticking clock hanging over their heads. "What will I ever do to repay you?"

He lifted her into his arms with a growl, the dress flowing to the floor in a wash of iridescent silk. "We'll think of something."

They did, and an hour later she was surprised when he rose from the bed in all his naked glory and put on jeans.

"Don't we have to get ready for the party?" she asked, her body loose and spent from the three orgasms Nico had delivered to her with his tongue, his fingers, his cock. It had been a delicious kind of denial, and one she'd desperately needed. Her mind felt clearer, and she was ready to get back to work.

"In a couple of hours," he said. "There's something I want to do first. But you'll need to get dressed."

Twenty minutes later, he was leading her through Locke's house to the wine cellar. "This might not be the best time for a wine tasting," she said.

"Funny," he said, leading her through the room to a big door. "But we're not going to drink wine." He pulled a key from the pocket of his jeans and inserted it into the lock.

"Then what are we doing?"

He opened the door and reached in to flip on some lights. A moment later, she stepped into a full size shooting gallery. At least, that's what she assumed it was. She'd only ever seen them on TV and in the movies.

"We're going to shoot," he said.

"We're going to shoot," she repeated, turning to look at him. "Guns?"

He sighed. "We could try slingshots, but guns will be more effective, I think."

She crossed her arms over her chest. "I'm not shooting a gun."

He touched a hand to her cheek, rubbed his thumb along her jawbone. "It's time for you to learn to protect yourself," he said. "I wish it wasn't, but it is."

She wanted to argue, but the regret in his eyes made her heart hurt. He didn't like that he had to do this, wouldn't do it if he didn't think it was necessary for her safety. And she trusted him, didn't she? Knew he would die to protect her?

"Okay," she said. "But I'm not crazy about the idea."

"That makes two of us," he said.

He led her to the end of the gallery and a rack of guns behind a cage. He used one of the keys on the ring to unlock the metal cage, then scanned the weapons on offer. After about a minute, he picked up a small handgun and checked the chamber. The weapon looked mean and cold in his hand, and she instinctively recoiled when he walked toward her with it.

He held it out. "Take it," he said. "It's not loaded. I just want you to get used to the feel of it in your hand."

She took it and was surprised by how heavy it was, how smooth and cold the alloy felt in her hand. A feeling of power rose within her, and she immediately squashed it. This wasn't power. This was violence. And she was only doing it to ease Nico's mind.

He explained that it would normally take several weeks of safety lessons before she would be cleared to shoot, but they didn't have that luxury now. She would have to learn the basics, and she would have to learn them fast. He took her through the pieces of the gun, showing her how to eject an empty clip and how to load a new one. He took special care explaining how the safety worked and cautioning her never to point it unless she meant to follow through by shooting.

When he was done, he walked away, returning a moment later with something that looked like old fashioned headphones.

"These will protect your hearing," he said, setting them carefully over her ears.

He got a pair for himself and maneuvered her to one of the firing lanes. At the end — too far away it seemed — was a target shaped like a person. He lined her up in the lane, moved behind her, and grasped her hips, telling her to widen her stance as he placed his big arms over her smaller ones. She hadn't realized she was shaking until he gently closed his hand over her forearms.

"Hey," he said. "It's okay. It's just a machine. Like a car or a lawnmower."

"A car or a lawnmower," she repeated.

"Exactly. Any difference comes from attributes you're assigning it." He paused. "Don't. It only has the power you give it. I'm going to teach you how to use it, and you'll see that there's nothing to be afraid of."

She took a deep breath. "Okay."

He explained how to raise her arms, how to hold them, how to line the target up in the gun's site. She followed his instructions, her heart beating like a trapped bird.

"Okay, now," he said, "when you're ready, take a nice, easy breath, and when you exhale, gently squeeze the trigger. Don't pull, just squeeze."

"Squeeze," she murmured.

She could feel his presence behind her, but she forced herself to focus on the target at the end of the lane. She inhaled, then let it out slowly and squeezed.

The gun bucked a little in her hand, and she heard the shot reverberating through the firing range even through the protective ear covering.

"Not bad for a first try," Nico said, coming to stand next to her.

She followed his gaze to the paper target. It took her a few seconds to find the tiny hole at the edge of the target's torso.

"Not bad?" she asked, her competitive spirit kicking in. "I barely hit it."

He turned to look at her, and she had to resist the urge to lean in, touch her lips to his. Her body felt supercharged with adrenaline, the gun sending some kind of primal message of danger to her brain. It was fucked up, but she couldn't deny it, and she wondered again if there was something primitive in humanity's DNA that got turned on in the face of danger.

Hurry up and propagate the spices before we all die.

He smiled. "Then try again."

She raised her arms, aimed, took a breath, let it out, and squeezed. This time the shot landed closer to the center of the target's torso.

"Nice," Nico said. "Again."

It took her twenty minutes to land a shot squarely in the chest of the target. Nico explained that she shouldn't bother aiming for the head if her life were threatened. It was too small a target, her odds of hitting it too small. Better to aim for the chest. Worse case, it would buy her some time.

Exhaustion swept over her all at once as Nico took the gun from her hands and locked it up in the cage. Her body had been firing on all cylinders, primed as if it were in real danger. Now she was crashing hard, her mind a swirl of conflicting emotions. She didn't like guns. Didn't like violence in general. She never had.

But she couldn't deny the power she'd felt holding the gun, power that came from knowing she could stop someone from hurting her. From hurting someone she loved.

How far would you go to protect the ones you love?

Until now she'd had the luxury of never having to ask herself the question. Now she wondered if she had it in her to do what was necessary to protect David, to protect Nico. To protect herself, too. She didn't know. She didn't know what was happening to her.

Nico wrapped an arm around her shoulders and guided her out of the room. When he'd locked the door, he turned to face her, his hands on her shoulders.

"I'm sorry," he said softly.

"For what?"

He shook his head. "For this. You wouldn't be here if it wasn't for me."

She sighed. "We can't do that, Nico. None of us knows where we'd be if things had turned out differently."

"Maybe," he said. "But you wouldn't be here."

"No, I'd be somewhere without you." She stood on tip toe to kiss him. "And that's somewhere I wouldn't want to be."

It was true, but it still didn't answer any of the questions in her head. What would happen to them when this was over? Could she live with Nico's business to have him in her life?

And would he even want her there?

22

"Angel... Time to wake up."

She was drifting in a pleasant darkness when Nico's voice pulled her clear of it. She sat up in the Porsche and looked around, taking in the landscaped grounds of a mid-century modern home in the Hollywood Hills. Palm trees dotted the front yard, illuminated with perfectly spaced lights and bordered with a stone pathway. Above them on a small hill, she could make out people milling around a living room inside the house, the faint sound of music a backdrop to their laughter.

"We're here," Nico said. "You slept the whole way."

She opened the compact in her purse and checked her makeup, glad she'd chosen to keep it simple with a bare face, eyeliner and mascara, and pale pink lipstick. She'd kept her hair simple, too, pulling it back into a low, sleek ponytail. Everything about LA was different from New York, including the makeup and fashion, and she'd learned how to navigate those differences when traveling with her father.

"I'm beat," she said.

"Will you be okay?" he asked, his brow furrowed with concern.

"I'll be fine."

He handed her something that looked like a modified flash drive. "Put this into the USB port on his computer. Sara's waiting in New York to install a backdoor on his system. It will only take her a minute to do it, but wait two minutes, just to be safe."

"Do I need to let her know once it's plugged in?"

"She'll know," he said. "It's programmed to connect immediately to her computer."

"And she'll be able to access his data with this?" Angel said.

"Barring some kind of serious security," he said. "And John doesn't strike me as very tech-savvy."

"What else should I look for?" she asked.

"Papers, files, anything that won't take too long and won't get you into trouble. But that stuff is all secondary to the computer, because if we have that, we have everything, even his phone assuming he backs up online."

She took a deep breath and slipped the device into her purse. "Got it."

"It'll be okay." He took her hand, rubbing his thumb along her palm in a gesture that lit a fuse between her legs. She tamped it down, wondering what was wrong with her. She was not the kind of person to be turned on by taking risks. Especially not risks like this one. "I'll make sure you're covered until you're done."

"I trust you," she said.

"You do?"

"I do," she whispered, surprised to realize it was true.

An expression of worry crossed his face before he managed to hide it. "Let's do it."

He came around to open her door and they started up a winding pathway to the house, awash with light at the top of the hill. The dress swirled around her legs in a delicious tumble of silk, and the warm night air caressed her exposed décolleté. She wished that just once, she and Nico could be dressed up to do something normal — not to have dinner in hiding at the Hudson Valley house or stay under the radar in Miami or plan the theft of intellectual property in Los Angeles.

At this point, dinner and a movie would be nice. Or even movies on the couch with a bowl of popcorn. She tried to imagine Nico doing something so normal. It wasn't as difficult as she expected, and she felt a pang of loss when she remembered that she probably wouldn't be the one to do those things with him.

The door was opened by a small man with dark hair and delicate features. Nico greeted him by name, and Angel realized this was John Lando. Everything Nico had said about him made sense; with his linen pants and open collared tunic, he was more movie executive than mob boss. And it wasn't just his clothes. He had a skittish air about him that made Angel think he was way out of his element, even here in his own home.

"This is Angel," Nico said, introducing them.

"I can see that," John said, kissing her hand and trying to be charming. Her stomach turned over as she returned his smile. This was someone who might know where David was being held. Who might be helping Dante.

And that made John Lando every bit the scum Dante was.

They made their way into John's house, past a crowd of people in the living room to the bar that was set up in what looked like a media room. A group of well-heeled people were sitting in the movie-theater style seats watching Taxi Driver on a big screen at the front of the room. Angel thought she recognized Elizabeth Kramer, an A-list actress, and a few other movie people, but she kept her focus on the house, letting her eyes roam the layout while Nico talked to John.

John got them each a drink and led them back out into the living room where he introduced them to a producer Angel had never heard of and a tall, lithe blond woman that looked vaguely familiar. John excused himself a moment later. She and Nico made small talk with their new acquaintances until Nico took her arm, saying they were going to look for food.

He led her to a table groaning with shrimp, sushi, fruit, and more finger food than Angel had fingers. Nico handed her a plate and started piling food on top of it while he spoke under his breath.

"There's a big guy with a mustache standing in front of the hallway," he said softly. "That's Gino Carelli, John's Underboss."

She turned with the plate of food, popping a shrimp in her mouth while she scanned the room, looking bored. She passed over Gino when she spotted him, not wanting to draw attention to herself, but her stomach coiled into a knot at the sight of him.

Gino was no John Lando. At least six-four, he had arms that were as thick as tree trunks, beady eyes, and a scowl that reminded her too much of Dante. His jeans and leather jacket left no doubt that he couldn't have cared less about the movie business.

He was obviously here on family business.

"He's here to keep an eye on me," Nico said. "Lucky for us, it looks like he's the only one."

Angel ate something that looked like a mini-crab cake. "If you say so."

"I'm going to say hello," he said. "Stay here."

She placed her free hand on his forearm. "Nico…"

He covered her fingers with his own without looking at her. "It's okay. Mingle. Act like you're happy to be here. We'll give Gino some time to let down his guard before we make our move."

He walked over to Gino, extending his arm to shake the other man's hand. Gino did not look happy to see him, and Nico played along, exhibiting a careful mix of familiarity and reserve. It was smart. If Gino was running the west coast family, he would be intuitive enough to be suspicious if Nico were too friendly, especially under the circumstances.

Nico was keeping it real.

Angel did the same, picking up her champagne glass and moving away from the table of food. She talked to actors and set designers, movie editors and musicians, even a marine biologist who was consulting on a film about deep sea exploration. It wasn't as difficult as she'd imagined. She asked a lot of questions, let everyone else do the talking so she could nod and smile while they talked about their favorite subject — themselves. It left her mind free to observe the house, to keep an eye on Gino and John, to notice the way Gino's eyes followed Nico wherever he went.

After about two hours, Nico appeared at her side while she was talking to a group of people not much older than her. They were looking for funding for a small indie film they were producing, and Angel found that she was interested in spite of the circumstances.

"Let's go outside, darling. I think John's pool is like the one you were talking about for the house in Miami."

Darling? She resisted the urge to roll her eyes.

Angel extricated herself from the conversation and walked with Nico to the patio on the other side of the kitchen. It was magnificent, set on the edge of the hill, nestled into the landscape with natural rock borders and a small waterfall. The lights of Los Angeles glimmered in the distance.

Nico led her to the edge of the patio and turned his back on the house, making it look like they were checking out the scenery.

"Gino's on edge," he said. "I think we're good."

"Please tell me why that's good," she said though clenched teeth.

"Because I've made a point of being nosy. He's on guard now — but only with me. I'm going to head out the front alone. He'll come after me when he sees that you're staying inside."

"What if he thinks you're going to the car or something?" she asked.

"He won't risk it. For all he knows, I'm trying to sneak back into the house through a window."

She took a deep breath, trying to slow the surge of adrenaline running through her body. "Okay."

"Head to the bathroom as soon as I leave," Nico said. "Make sure the hall's clear and try the third closed door on the right. It should be John's office."

"Should be?"

He shrugged. "I asked John for the number of a mutual acquaintance. That's where he went to get it. It's the best I can do. And it doesn't matter if I'm wrong, because John is posturing with Hollywood royalty and I'll be keeping Gino busy. No one else here gives a shit."

She nodded, trying to calm her nerves. "Got it."

He reached for her hand. "You don't have to do this."

"Yes, I do," she said. "David's out there with Dante. If we don't save him, no one will."

"We'll find another way."

"What way?"

He sighed. "I don't know."

"Then this is the way," she said. "It'll be fine. Like you said; you'll keep Gino busy. I'll check John's office."

"Okay, but keep an ear out for John. He'll still be inside at the party."

She thought of the diminutive man who'd opened the door to them. "I can take care of John if I have to."

He scowled. "Just get out safe, Angel. That's all."

She kissed his cheek. "I'll be fine. Now go."

He stared at her for a long minute. She knew from the look in his eyes that he wanted to kiss her, but a moment later, he went inside.

She looked around to make sure no one was watching, then dumped her champagne over the edge of the patio and returned to the house with her empty glass.

23

Everyone was talking, laughing, maybe a little drunk. They'd gotten comfortable, and someone had turned the music up.

Good.

She set her glass on the bar, watching in her peripheral vision as Nico headed outside. Gino was on his heels before he'd even shut the door behind him.

Angel picked up her newly refilled glass and headed for the hall, trying to look casual. She had her hand on the bathroom door when she felt a tap on her shoulder. She froze, then turned slowly, half-expecting Gino to be staring her down.

It was a woman in a long black dress, her red hair styled in a braid that hung over one shoulder. "Is there another one?"

"Excuse me?" Angel asked.

"Another restroom."

Angel almost cried with relief. "I think so." She stepped away from the door. "Here, take this one."

"Are you sure?" the redhead asked.

Angel smiled. "Totally. I think there's another one down the hall."

"Thanks," the woman said. "All this champagne."

Angel laughed, lifting her glass a little. "Agreed."

She waited for the woman to close the bathroom door, then continued down the hall. She turned the knob to the third door on the right, half-expecting it to be locked. It wasn't, and she slipped quietly into the room.

The lights were off, but a faint glow lit the room from the pool and patio on the other side of curtained glass doors. She took a minute to look around, getting her bearings.

Sofa, two chairs, coffee table, desk.

Laptop on desk.

She hurried over to it and opened the computer, careful to stay out of the light seeping in from outside. The pool was around the corner of the house, but she didn't want to risk having her silhouette spotted by someone looking for a moment of quiet or a couple searching for a private place for a hook up.

She marked the time on the display as the computer came to life.

12:02

There was a password screen, and she inserted the device Nico had given her and watched as the System Preferences window opened as if by magic. A second later an empty search bar appeared. Letters and numbers started moving across it, some invisible hand (Sara in New York?) using the device to take control of John's computer. Just when she thought the show was over, a black screen popped up, and some kind of code scrolled quickly across the surface.

12:03

She was close, so close, to something that might lead her to David.

Something rattled by the glass door, and she ducked, moving farther out of the light, her heart feeling like it would beat out of her chest.

"Trust me," a male voice said outside the door. "John won't mind."

The knob rattled as they started to enter the room.

Shit, shit, shit!

She looked at the computer. The code was still scrolling, and it was still 12:03.

"Looks like it's locked," a different male voice said. "Too bad."

"This patio wraps all the way around the house," the first voice said, growing fainter. "Let's see if…"

Angel exhaled, holding a hand to her chest. She looked back at the computer.

12:04.

The computer looked just like it had when she'd first opened it.

She removed the mystery device from the USB port, and shoved it in her purse. Then she closed the computer and moved for the door. She was almost there when it opened.

"What are you doing in here?" John Lando asked, his eyes narrow with suspicion.

"Looking for a bathroom," Angel said. "I was going to use the one in the hall, but someone needed it. Pretty redhead? Tall?"

He studied her. "You're Carlo Rossi's daughter."

It sounded like an accusation, but that was probably her own baggage. She lifted her chin. She wasn't going to let this coward make her feel bad about her father.

"Yes."

He walked toward her, stopped a little too close. He wasn't tall, but then neither was she. They were almost eye to eye, and while she wasn't intimidated by him per se, she was very aware of Gino somewhere on the property — and equally aware that he wasn't some mild-mannered studio executive playing Mob Boss in a movie.

"You're with the man who killed your father?" John asked, referring to Nico.

"We have mutual business concerns," she said.

She saw his eyes light with interest. "Is that so?"

"It is." She met his eyes, held his gaze. "Excuse me. I should be getting back."

He didn't move at first, and she thought he might call Gino after all. But a few seconds later, he stepped aside, gesturing for her to go ahead.

She walked as calmly as she could to the living room. When she didn't see Nico, she headed for the front door, holding her breath every step of the way.

24

"I can't believe you stole John's car," Angel laughed.

"It's a nice car," Nico said as they drove up the driveway toward Locke's house. "And I didn't steal it. I took it for a test drive."

Nico had hot-wired John's Audi and was pulling down the driveway when Gino ran outside. He hadn't been worried about Gino calling the police. Angel was still inside, and Nico had seen more than one party guest snorting coke. It wasn't uncommon in Hollywood, but that didn't mean John wanted to see it on TMZ.

By the time Angel emerged from the house, Nico was speeding up the driveway, tucking the car back into its parking place at the top of the path. Gino had tried to take a shot at him with a weak left hook when Nico got out of the car, but he had easily deflected it.

It was official; California soldiers were soft.

There had been some commotion with John when he'd found out about Nico's test drive, but what could he do? The car had been returned safe and sound. He'd apologized and they'd made a hasty exit.

Nico wasn't worried that John had caught Angel in his office. They'd search it, see if anything was missing. But nothing would be, and Sara's access to John's computer through the DriveHacker would be untraceable to all but the most experienced of security experts.

"Do you really think Sara will find something to lead us to David?" Angel asked as Nico pulled to a stop in front of Locke's house.

His breath caught in his throat as he turned toward her. He never got tired of looking at her, was fascinated by the way her face seemed to change depending on her clothes, the way she wore her hair, how she was feeling that day. She was a mystery he wanted to spend a lifetime trying to solve, and tonight her eyes looked bigger and greener than usual, her cheekbones pronounced under the simple ponytail that somehow managed to be sexy as hell. He hated the worry in her voice, hated that he'd made her a party to the darkest side of his world.

He took her hand. "I hope so."

She looked out the window. "Seventy-two hours tomorrow."

"I know," he said, her sadness like a vise around his heart.

"What will I tell Dante when he calls?"

He squeezed her hand. "We'll figure something out. Sara's going to work through the night. Maybe she'll have something by then."

"Maybe," Angel said softly.

They went inside, and Angel slipped off her shoes while Nico poured them both a glass of wine. He nodded to the patio.

"Shall we?"

She nodded, taking the glass he offered, and they sat on the edge of the pool, resting their bare feet on the second step.

"You know," she said, "that wasn't as bad I thought it would be."

"Contemplating a life of crime?" he asked.

Her laughter was deep and throaty, and he felt himself grow hard in response. It was the way she laughed in bed, right after he'd teased her, tasted her, made her come.

"Hardly," she said. "I don't think I'm cut out for it."

"I'm glad to hear it." He wasn't at all kidding.

She took a long drink of her wine, then surprised him by standing and unzipping her dress. She let it fall to the stone, and he saw that she was naked underneath, hadn't been wearing underwear all night. She shook out the ponytail, letting her long hair fall to her waist in a cascade of waves.

His cock stood at full attention as she walked languidly to the deep end, arcing into the water with hardly a splash. He watched as she made his way toward him underwater, her bare body illuminated by the pool light. She came up in front of him and smoothed her hair back from her face, then touched his feet underwater.

"You don't think criminals are sexy?" she asked, continuing their conversation as if she hadn't just prevented his brain from thinking about anything but burying himself between her legs.

"I think you're sexy," he said.

She reached for his belt. "The feeling is mutual."

She unzipped his pants, releasing his cock and taking it in her hand. The feel of her cool palm on his sensitive flesh made him harder. He recognized the shine in her eyes, the manic energy lurking there. It was a danger high, and he'd had plenty of experience with it. In a life or death confrontation, the body was primed and pumped, hell bent on its own survival. It took a while for all that energy to dissipate after the threat had passed. When it did, it was a hell of a crash, but until then, Nico had found the only cures to be working out and fucking.

And he had no plans to visit Locke's gym with Angel.

She stroked his shaft, working her way in between his legs until she could reach him with her mouth. He couldn't have cared less about the fact that she was getting his pants wet as she leaned in, flicking her tongue against his tip.

He reached out, pinching her erect nipples as she closed her mouth around his head, tonguing him at the top until he had to fight the urge to thrust his hips upward.

"Angel..."

She dipped her tongue into the hole at his tip while she sucked, then slid down the length of him, taking him in her mouth. She had every inch of him captive, and she grasped the base of his cock while she moved over his shaft, working him like she always did, knowing exactly what he wanted, and exactly how.

When he couldn't stand it anymore, he put his hands on either side of her head and forced her to look at him. She needed to burn off the adrenaline coursing through her veins, and she wasn't going to do that by giving him a blow job — even if it was the best blow job of all time.

He stood, dropping his pants and stripping off his shirt.

"What are you doing?" she asked, looking up at him, her eyes bright with lust. She was as breathless for him as he was for her. He could see it in the quick rise and fall of her chest, her perfect breasts glistening with water in the light of the pool.

"I'm getting ready to lick your pussy until you come," he said. "And then I'm going to fuck you until you come again."

"Where are you going?"

He ignored the question, walking to the deep end of the pool, giving her the same show she'd given him. The truth was, he needed some time to cool off. If he let her touch him again now, he was going to come. And he wasn't planning on doing that until he'd taken care of her.

He dove in, the water sliding against his naked body as he swam toward her. He could see her bare legs on the pool step. He came up between them, kneeled on the step in front of her. She was his nirvana, his addiction, and his goddess, and he would gladly worship at the altar of her body until the day he died.

He put his hand at the back of her head, pulled her toward him, plunged his tongue into her mouth. She was just as eager, and she slid her arms around his naked body, the water slipping between them as she swept his mouth with her tongue, pressing her body to his like she couldn't get close enough. Finally he pulled back, looking her in the eyes as he lowered himself into the water in front of her and spread her legs.

The water lapped gently against the folds of her sex, and he leaned in, closing his mouth all at once over her pussy, cold from the water. She cried out, arching her back for him, pushing against the warmth of his mouth. He kept it tight against her, covering her with his tongue, sucking her clit until she moaned, moving her hips in time to his rhythm.

He slid two fingers into her as her orgasm built. The feel of her tightening around him sent a bolt of lightning to his cock. He could almost feel himself there, feel her clenching around him as he pushed into her. He needed to be inside her. Needed to feel her come for him while he took possession of her body, while he drove out all the bad things that had brought them to this place.

He sucked harder and pressed a finger against the blossom of her asshole.

"Oh….oh, god, Nico…" she gasped. "Please… I can't…."

He lifted his mouth from her while he stroked and pressed. "You can't what, baby? You can't stand it?" He lapped at the glistening petals of her sex. "It feels good, doesn't it?"

"Yes… Oh, god, yes…"

"Then come for me, baby," he said. "Come while I eat your pussy. And then come again when I fuck you."

He closed his mouth around her clit and sucked, pressing harder against the perfect circle of her ass. He knew the moment she tipped over the edge. She shuddered, her body tightening against his fingers, his mouth, her hips lifting as she sought to get closer to his mouth, needing him to consume her as much as he needed to consume her.

When the last vestiges of her orgasm had passed, he knelt between her legs, grabbing for his pants to get a condom. She leaned back on her arms, her eyes glassy.

"I want it, Nico."

He positioned himself at her opening and looked in her eyes. "Tell me what you want, Angel."

She didn't look away. "I want you to fuck me."

He pushed into her just a little. "Like this?"

She moaned, arching her back. "Fuck… please. I need it."

"You need what?" he asked, pushing into her a little more.

"I need your cock inside me, Nico. All of it."

He leaned over her wet, naked body and thrust his tongue into her mouth while he drove into her. She cried out, and he felt his cock grow harder still. Then he was thrusting and driving, somewhere else entirely, in a place where there was nothing but Angel's warm body enveloping him, welcoming every inch as he plunged into her, taking her with a ferocity she seemed to demand as she met his thrusts, grabbing his ass and driving him all the way inside of her.

He reached down with one hand and stroked her clit while he took her, and he felt her begin the climb all over again, his own body matching stride, keeping pace until she screamed. Her body tightened around him as she came, and he poured himself into her, still driving, wanting to get everything out of her, wanting to give her every bit of him.

They collapsed together, Angel slumping against the pool step while her hands dove into his hair. He pulled her down into the water with him, cradling her body in the water. He stroked the hair back from her face as she rested her head against his shoulder.

"Now you'll sleep."

25

The sky was still dark when her phone rang on the nightstand the next morning. She was immediately awake, and she sat up, and pressed the button to accept the call with one hand while she nudged Nico with the other.

"I hope I didn't wake you," Dante said on the other end of the phone. He sounded almost pleasant, like they were old friends.

"I'm awake," she said, waving away Nico's hand as he reached for her phone.

"I hope it's because you're keeping Nico company while he makes plans to hand over the New York territory to me."

Fear clutched at her chest. This was it; the moment she'd been dreading. The moment when she would have to rely on Dante's non-existent empathy to buy more time for David.

"I need more time," she said.

"That wasn't our deal."

"I know, she said. "But I… it's not as easy as you think it is. Nico won't give up the territory. Not even for - "

"Not even for you?" he finished.

"Not even for me." Resentment sucker punched her from behind, and she immediately shoved it aside. Stupid. She knew Nico was doing everything he could to rescue David, and she didn't want him to give up the territory for Dante.

He was messing with her. Getting under her skin.

"Must be tough to fuck him knowing he doesn't give a shit about your brother."

She took a deep breath, let it out slowly, forced her voice steady. "Can you give me a couple more days?"

He didn't say anything right away, and for a minute she thought he'd hung up.

"Go to the Ripley's museum in Hollywood tomorrow at six pm," he finally said. "There will be a gift shop bag on the floor near the Human Salamander."

"The Human Salamander?"

"Am I speaking Chinese?" She jumped as he shouted into the phone. She heard him take a deep breath, like he was trying to gain control of his temper. "Just go there. You'll know it when you see it."

"Okay," she said, torn between being relieved that he seemed willing to negotiate and freaked out by his choice of meeting places. "Is... is my brother okay?"

"Coming alone gives you a better shot at that," he said. "Tomorrow. Six pm."

He hung up before she could say anything else.

She set her phone down, and Nico kneeled on the floor in front of her, taking her shaking hands in his.

"He wants you to meet him?"

"Yes... no... I don't know." She got up, pacing the floor. "He wants me to come to the Ripley's Museum in Hollywood tomorrow at six."

Nico's eyes registered surprise. "Ripley's?"

She nodded. "At the Human Salamander."

Nico exhaled his rage, and his eyes turned cold. "What a sick fuck."

"He said there would be a bag waiting for me with instructions."

"With instructions?" Nico asked. "He used those exact words?"

She nodded. "And he said to come alone."

"He can say it all he wants," Nico said, his voice threatening. "There's no way in hell I'm letting you within a mile of that asshole alone."

"You have to," she said. "David's life might depend on it."

"I can't do it, Angel." He left the room, headed for the kitchen.

She followed him, watching as he started to make coffee.

"You don't get to make this decision, Nico." She wedged herself between him and the counter, forced him to look at her. "Not this one."

"I can't risk it," he said. "I can't risk you."

"Dante could have killed me a long time ago. He needs me free to get what he wants."

"I don't like it." His amber eyes were almost feral.

She reached up to hold his face in her hands. "I don't like it, either. But you have to do this for me."

His eyes turned cold, and she knew he was doing what he always did in a tough situation; weighing the odds, calculating, looking for the best answer in a field of shitty ones.

"We watch you come and go from the street," he said.

She shook her head. "If he sees you, he might kill David."

"And if he takes you, how will you help your brother?"

She hesitated. He was right. She knew it, she just didn't want to believe it.

"How can we be sure he won't see you?"

"He won't," Nico said. "That much I can promise you."

The steel running through his voice told her all she needed to know. "Fine. But you have to stay out of sight. We can't afford to piss him off. David can't afford it."

"You have my word," he said.

She nodded. "Who's we?" she said, remembering his choice of words. "You said '*We* watch you come and go from the street.'"

He met her eyes. "I said I'd keep you safe, Angel, and that's what I intend to do. Even if it takes an army to do it."

26

They sat at the table, drinking coffee and pouring over the reports from Sara's search results until the sun started lightening the sky. Then they went for a swim in the ocean below the house. It was cleansing, and Angel emerged from the water feeling calmer and more centered.

Luca arrived before noon, accompanied by two gargantuan men named Marco and Elia, and Sara Falco, the hacker who had been working behind the scenes to find information on Dante's location. Angel had been surprised by the entourage until she remembered Nico's words the night before. The army he was deploying was small — for now — but she had no doubt he would call in as many people as possible to keep her safe.

"The problem with Ripley's," Marco said after Nico had briefed everyone, "is that you can't see shit once someone's inside. I don't think there's a single window past the lobby."

He was huge, but she had gotten used to that — Nico seemed to surround himself by men big enough to break the average person in half with their bare hands — but it was his eyes that got her attention. Cool and gray with the steady gaze of a man who didn't let much deter him, they told her everything she needed to know about why Nico had included him on the team. He wore his black hair shaved close to the head. Angel wondered if he'd been in the military.

"I'm aware," Nico said tightly. "Which is why I want the exits locked down."

"Can we wire her?" Elia asked. His arms were twice the size of Angel's waist, his head shaved to expose a gleaming pate.

"She won't let us do that," Nico said at the same time Angel said, "No."

Elia sighed, his struggle not to roll his eyes obvious.

"She's protecting her brother," Sara said softly. "If Dante frisks her and finds a wire, David is in trouble."

Angel looked gratefully at the other woman. Steeped in testosterone since the day she'd gone to Maine to help Nico, Angel had been happy to see the other woman step into the room with Luca and the others. Sara was tall and slim, with hair the color of a new penny and eyes that were pale green, the exact color of the foamy water that washed onto the beach below Locke's house. She had a soft, gentle energy that made it hard to imagine her as the hard core hacker Angel knew she was.

"We understand that," Nico said. "But she's not going to do David any good if something happens to her."

"I get it," Sara said. "But it doesn't make sense for Dante to hurt her."

It was exactly the thing Angel had been telling Nico since Dante's call, and she was relieved to have someone from the family saying the same thing. It wasn't that Nico didn't trust her judgement; it was that his feelings for her blinded him. She understood it. She could hardly think clearly with her fear for David lurking in her mind. And she'd proven Nico's well-being was as important to her as her own the minute she'd gotten in the car and driven to Maine.

"You're acting like Dante is reasonable," Luca said. "He isn't. A rabid animal doesn't bite just to protect itself. It bites to satisfy an impulse."

"I know that, Luca." Angel wondered if she was imagining the way Sara spoke Luca's name — like it held the weight of something unspoken between them. "But I think it's a safe assumption right now that Angel will be okay. And it's not like we have a choice."

"She's right," Nico said. "Let's not rehash it. Let's just make sure we're ready for anything."

"I have the files from John's computer," Sara said. "How do you want them?"

"Can you encrypt them and send them to me?" Nico asked her.

She nodded. "I haven't gotten very far cross-referencing them with the search string from Carlo Rossi's office, but I'll start that later today when we get back."

"You're coming, too?" Angel asked.

Sara looked surprised. "I thought Nico told you."

"We need someone inside, Angel," he said. "Someone who has eyes on you, just in case."

"He said to come alone," Angel said, unable to hide the anger in her voice. "We talked about this."

"Sara has never been part of a tactical team," Nico said. "No one knows she works for us. She'll look like a tourist, and she'll give you plenty of breathing room."

Angel stalked to the edge of the patio. "This wasn't our deal."

"It is now," Nico said, his voice low. "You're just going to have to trust me here, Angel."

She turned around and looked at Sara. She looked like any average woman off the street. If Nico insisted on sending someone in with her, Sara was probably a best case scenario. She was definitely better than one of the muscled behemoths that made up the tactical team.

"Okay," she said, deciding to quit fighting while she was ahead.

"Good," Nico said. "Now let's gear up. We should leave by two-thirty so we can get into position before any of Dante's men arrive."

They went over a map of the area around the museum, and Angel watched as Nico marked the places where they'd be set up to watch the entrances and exits. As soon as they started talking weaponry, she decamped with Sara to the kitchen. It wasn't that she didn't care or that the tactical planning wasn't interesting, but she didn't want to think about all the firepower aimed her way while she was trying to follow Dante's instructions. She was already on edge, wondering if David was okay, if Dante might be about to relent and let her see her brother as some kind of incentive to keep working on Nico.

And then there was the other thing she kept thinking. That Nico was right. That Dante was an animal, ruled by violent impulse instead of logic.

But no. She wouldn't let herself think about that. Sara was right; David was her only incentive to do what Dante wanted her to do. Without him, Dante was done. He had to know that Nico would set the city on fire looking for him then.

"Are you okay?" Sara asked, when they were alone in the kitchen.

Angel pulled bread, milk, and eggs from the fridge to make French toast. Sara and the others had to be jet-lagged, and Angel was starting to feel the effects of her sleepless night. They would all need to be alert. Food would help. So would more coffee.

"Yeah," Angel said, starting a fresh pot of coffee to brew while she cooked. "Just... you know... scared."

Sara nodded. "For what it's worth, these guys know what they're doing. I know it's scary, but there's no one I would trust more if I were in your situation."

Angel met her eyes. "Really?"

Sara smiled. "Really."

Angel exhaled, and the fist around her heart loosened just a little. "Thanks."

"Sure," Sara said. "Now let me help. These guys eat like you wouldn't believe."

27

They caravanned to Hollywood in two of Locke's SUVs and arrived with plenty of time to spare. Angel rode with Nico, both of them tense and silent as they left the freeway behind and entered into the sprawling metropolis that was the LA metro area.

Nico hated that she had to do this. Hated that there was no other way. But she was right; doing anything but following Dante's instructions was risky, and he couldn't take another risk with a member of Angel's family. Couldn't live with it if something went wrong and she blamed him.

She was making him soft. At least where she was concerned. He'd gotten used to living only for himself and the legacy left to him by his father. It had been easy, simple. He did what was best for the business. He tried to do it with minimal damage to others, tried to keep innocents out of the mix. But if push came to shove, he did what was best for the family.

This new vulnerability left him with a complex storm of emotion. He didn't do vulnerable. But he wanted Angel. Wanted her body, her heart, her soul. He could no longer imagine what his life would be like without her.

Scratch that; he could, and it looked fucking miserable.

It turned out that loving someone and keeping them safe within the confines of his work wasn't easy. He had new respect for his father. Despite his mistakes, he'd made Nico and his mother feel safe and loved. Had taught Nico strength and honor, two attributes that didn't always seem to go hand in hand. Would he be able to do the same if he stayed with Angel?

He glanced over at her, staring out the window as the streets of Hollywood passed by on the other side of the glass. His chest squeezed, and he recognized the sensation as the increasingly familiar one of love for her. She was brave and good, stronger than she gave herself credit for. He would protect her at any cost, see her safely out of this mess, and her brother, too.

He would.

He drove toward the museum, making sure to keep Luca and the others in sight in the rearview mirror. He wanted Angel to know what the building looked like, wanted to remove any additional stress that might be caused by worrying that she had the right place.

"Right there," he said as they passed the squat building near the corner. "You see it?"

She nodded.

He drove half a mile out of their way to park. If playing Dante's game was the only way to make sure David stayed safe until they could figure out where Dante was keeping him, Nico could at least make sure Dante didn't know Angel was being followed.

He looked over at her. "You okay?"

She nodded.

"We can tell this guy to go fuck himself, you know," he said softly.

"No, we can't. Not while he has David."

He hated that she was right. He thought about all the firepower they'd brought to make himself feel better. They'd mapped out the most ideal locations to keep an eye on the exits, and he'd given himself the location closest to the museum. He figured he could be inside in less than a minute if Sara signaled him with her headset, and with the others covering the exits, Dante wouldn't get out alive.

Of course, they couldn't make a move if Dante didn't hurt Angel first, and Nico had to tamp down the rage at the reminder of their very limited options. Either Dante would just fuck with her, in which case they had to let him out alive to ensure David's safety, or Dante would hurt her, in which case killing him would be cold comfort to Nico.

They pulled into a parking place, neither of them moving as the car went quiet. There was so much to say, and he didn't trust himself to say any of it. He didn't want to frighten her with last words. Didn't want to make her think he was afraid, even though losing her was the one and only thing that scared the shit out of him.

He reached for her hand, squeezed, and got out of the car.

28

Angel watched as Luca and the others piled out of the second SUV. Sara moved off to the side while the men unloaded two big duffel bags from the back. Angel swallowed her dread. She knew the bags were loaded with weapons, but she couldn't afford to think about it. Couldn't afford to care.

She'd been numb when Nico first turned off the freeway and headed toward downtown Hollywood. It had been nice, pleasant, and for a while she thought it wouldn't be so bad. She'd meet Dante, and then she'd go back to Nico with new information that would help them find David.

But then she'd looked up, spotting Griffith Observatory perched on a hill above the city. She'd had a sudden memory of sitting in the planetarium with David, both of them tipped back in their seats, staring at the three dimensional rendering of the cosmos over their heads. She'd turned to say something to David and had been stopped cold by his rapt expression as he'd stared upward. He'd looked so young, so awed by the display, that she'd taken his hand and turned her own eyes back to the ceiling without saying a word. Maybe they would go back when this was all over. Hold hands in the dark and try to turn back the clock to a time when seeming small and powerless had meant comfort instead of fear.

The men collected their stuff and turned to leave without a word, all except for Luca who gave her a quick hug. "Deep breaths, Angel. We have your back."

What about David's back? she thought.

She didn't say it. She had David's back. And she would do anything to have him returned safely.

How far would you go to protect the ones you love?

"Thanks, Luca."

He glanced at Sara, his gaze lingering briefly on her face before he turned to join the others. Then Angel and Nico were alone, or as alone as they could be with traffic speeding behind them and a city full of tourists.

"You know what to do?" Nico asked her.

"Walk to the museum," she said. "Sara will be following me at a distance, but I shouldn't look back. Go to the Human Salamander exhibit. Don't glance around. Don't look for you. Don't do anything that would make someone think I'm being followed."

Nico nodded. "Do what you need to do and get out."

His voice was calm, but the tempest in his eyes scared her. He was not a man who was used to being backed into a corner. He was choosing his movements carefully, resisting the urge to tear the city apart looking for Dante, but she was worried for him. Worried that when he was finally free to act, the Los Angeles family — and maybe Nico's, too — would be nothing but ash.

"I will."

He crushed her to him. "I'll be right outside, and I'll be watching."

She nodded against his chest, then pulled away. "See you soon."

She started walking.

The sun had sunk below the horizon. Lights lit up Hollywood Boulevard, casting red and blue and yellow lights onto the pavement. A steady stream of cars moved down the street, and Angel weaved her way around the throngs of people enjoying the warm spring night as she headed toward the Ripley's museum. She didn't know if Dante was watching her, but Sara was somewhere behind her, and she had no doubt that Nico was watching her every move. She was scared for David's safety. Maybe even a little sacred for her own.

But she wasn't alone.

She looked around, taking in the busy scene around her as she tried to calm her mind. Tourists took pictures outside of Grauman's Chinese and next to stars on the Walk of Fame, while LA's casually stylish residents entered the boutiques on Melrose.

She didn't care about any of it. She wanted to get her brother and return to New York. Turn her back on all of the ugliness associated with the Syndicate's business.

She was surprised when she finally came upon the museum, although "museum" was probably a stretch. Housed in a bland, nondescript building with a giant dinosaur poking out of the roof, it looked more like a fast food restaurant than a museum. The sign out front read RIPLEY'S BELIEVE IT OR NOT ODDITOREUM. Apparently the people in marketing at Ripley's thought "museum" was a stretch, too.

She forced herself not to look around in case someone was watching. Then she took a deep breath and walked through the doors.

29

The lobby was just as boring as the exterior of the building. After a brief hesitation (should she wait in the lobby? go inside?), she bought a ticket from a bald man at the booth and stepped through a metal turnstile.

She entered a small room with linoleum flooring and low ceilings. It looked almost carnival-esque, with glass display cases lining the walls and colorful posters and signs pointing to the various exhibits. She stopped at each of them, lingering, trying to look like a tourist. She didn't want to do anything that might spook Dante or piss him off.

A quote from Robert Ripley was painted on a wall in the middle of the room.

"I have traveled 201 countries and the strangest thing I've seen is man."

It was oddly appropriate, and the words echoed in her mind as she stopped at a display showcasing a shrunken head. According to the description on the placard, a South American tribe was known for taking the heads of their fallen enemies, removing the skin, and shrinking the heads as a kind of trophy.

She shuddered, and Dante's choice of meeting place took on an even more ominous air.

She continued to a case holding an authentic vampire killing kit. Using the glass as a mirror, she tried to case the room behind her without being obvious, looking for signs of Sara or Dante. She didn't see either of them, and she wondered if Sara had been waylaid or if she was just really good at staying out of sight.

She reached the back of the room and followed a narrow ramp downward to a level below ground. It had the air of a fun house, and there was something surreal and a little twisted about the warren of rooms, garish displays, and too bright colors of the posters.

The room was empty, and she started with a seemingly innocuous motorcycle crafted entirely out of candy. She stood there for a moment, forcing herself to breathe calm and slow before moving on.

The room was gray and dimly lit, with shadows creeping outward from the wall. The whole thing felt a little fucked up, and she had to fight panic as she stopped at a large, oddly shaped skeleton. The description said it was a cave bear, an extinct species of animal said to roam the earth over a hundred thousand years ago. It looked sad and lonely, and she suddenly wanted to take it out of here, bury it in the ground, let the earth reclaim it. That's where it should have been, not here on display like some kind of freak show.

She shook her head. She was getting morbid. The museum was strangely isolating, the basement level even more so than the first floor. She needed to find the Human Salamander display and get the hell out of here.

She wound her way down another small ramp to yet another level, and came out into another shadowed room with more display cases. Across the room, she recognized the Human Salamander display from her research on the internet.

Finally.

The museum was quiet. She had yet to see another person, and she wondered if it was sheer coincidence, or if Dante had begun to yield the same kind of power in LA that Nico yielded in New York. Had he paid someone to keep the museum empty? And if so, was Sara really behind her somewhere? Or had she been prevented from coming in?

Fear thrummed through her body along with a healthy dose of adrenaline. She forced her feet to keep moving toward the display, her entire being rebelling against the sight in front of her. It had looked fucked up on Locke's computer. Up close it was truly disturbing.

The display featured a waxy skinned man surrounded by brick and bent over at the waist, resting on all fours with his hands tied. His eyes seemed to bulge from their sockets, and an apple was stuck in his mouth.

She didn't see anything that might be from Dante — her brain rebelled against the idea that the display itself was some kind of message about David — so she turned her attention to the placard that explained the exhibit.

"Ian Chabert, a nineteenth century Parisian baker known as the "Human Salamander" could enter a blazing oven with two raw steaks and emerge unharmed even as the meat was well-cooked."

Her stomach turned over, and she turned around, expecting to see Dante standing behind her. But the room was empty, the museum still as quiet as a tomb.

She looked at the display, combing over it for the gift shop bag Dante had mentioned. He definitely had issues, but what would be the point in bringing her here, in arranging this twisted little field trip, if not to give her some kind of message?

She looked around the sides of the glass case, even peered behind it. But other than the man gaping at her like a roast pig, there was nothing unusual about the display.

She stepped back, willing her eyes to see the whole thing, to stop looking for something specific and let her brain do the work of telling her what was out of place. A moment later she saw it; a small white bag on top of the display case near the wall behind it.

She wedged herself in between the glass and the wall and reached up, her fingers finding nothing but dust in the seconds before they finally brushed against the smooth paper bag. Standing on tip toe, she stretched until she could close her hand around it and pull it down.

Her heart thudded in her chest, and she almost thought she could hear the blood rushing in her veins as she peered inside the bag, her gaze coming to rest on a small black box. She lifted it out and set the bag on the floor, then held her breath as she braced herself to open the metal box.

Her mind was already shouting a warning. But Dante had David. She had to know what was inside. She opened it slowly, her mind at first refusing to acknowledge the two charred fingers resting on a bed of red velvet, the note nestled in the box's lid that read BEHOLD THE EIGHT FINGERED MAN!!! HE CAN'T HOLD A PEN, BUT HE CAN STILL SUCK COCK!!!

And then she was screaming and screaming and screaming.

30

"She's asleep," Nico said, stepping out onto the patio.

"How is she?" Elia asked.

"Not fucking good," Nico said.

He was vaguely aware that he was slipping; loosening the reigns on protocol he'd introduced as part of the family's reboot. No swearing on the job, no losing your cool, personal business and family business kept separately at all times…. all maxims Nico was breaking with increasing frequency.

"Did the Xanax help?" Sara asked softly.

She sat close to Luca, and Nico tried to step back from the situation long enough to see if it was inappropriately close or in-solidarity-close. The last thing they needed was for Luca to have feelings for a member of the family. Especially a member who was involved in what was already a monumental nightmare. Nico would have to caution him.

"It did," Nico said. "Thanks for that."

Sara nodded. "I get nervous on planes."

Nico tried to smile. "Try a martini if you ever find yourself out of Xanax. Works just as good."

She nodded.

"What do we do now?" Marco asked.

The big man had been unusually quiet. Nico had chosen Marco and Elia for their loyalty, discretion, and unwavering stoicism. But the mind fuck Dante had perpetrated against Angel had worked on all of them, and it had taken obvious effort for the men to remain impassive when Sara brought her sobbing out of the museum. Take three of the most dangerous men in the world and put a crying woman in front of them — especially someone inherently vulnerable like Angel — and they turned to mush.

Now they knew that Dante meant business, and even if Angel got her brother back alive, he would be changed forever. So would she.

"Motherfucker!" Nico shouted, putting his fist through one of Locke's glass doors.

Everyone stood silent as they stared at the blood dripping from his hand onto the patio. "I'll get a towel." Sara hurried into the kitchen and returned with a dishtowel. She started to wrap it around Nico's hand, but he pulled it away from her and did the job himself. He didn't want anyone but Angel touching him, not even someone as nice as Sara Falco.

"I think you may need stitches for that, boss," Luca said, watching the blood seep through the towel.

"I'm fine," Nico said through his teeth.

He thought of the empty churches he used to sit in, their strange quiet, the proximity he'd felt to his mother and father. It was tempting, but he doubted anything could calm the storm raging in his mind. He pushed aside the fury that threatened to consume him, the desire to tear the city apart looking for Dante, to go in to John Lando's office shooting until the yellow-bellied coward told Nico what he knew. He needed to break the problem down in his head.

Emotion would get David killed. Reason might save him.

"Do whatever you have to do to get the security footage from the storefronts surrounding the museum," he said. "Traffic cams, too, if this godforsaken city has them."

"This isn't our territory," Luca said. "Should we go through John - "

"I don't give a…" Nico stopped himself, trying to reclaim the professionalism he'd worked to instill in the family in the two years before he met Angel. "Do not ask John's permission. Do not ask for Gino's permission. Just get the tapes by any means necessary. And get them today."

Luca nodded, then shuffled a little on his feet. It was uncharacteristic of him to show any kind of uncertainty. Something else was up.

"What is it, Luca?"

Luca exhaled. "It's Vincent."

"Vincent?"

Luca nodded. "He's gone."

"Can you be more specific?" Nico asked. But he already knew.

"He hasn't reported for work in two days, and he's not picking up his phone. Family claims not to know where he is."

Nico turned away, stared out over the water. It was beautiful, but it wasn't Maine, and he suddenly wished he and Angel were there, walking the craggy shoreline with nothing between them.

He could have gone through the motions of asking Luca questions, but it would be a waste of time. It was obvious what was happening; Vincent had defected to Dante's camp, was helping the bastard orchestrate a takedown of the New York family like all the other men he'd lost.

He was surprised to find he didn't care. The coup was an effort to stop the inevitable flow of change. Those who were attempting to do so would soon be obsolete — if not through Nico's efforts, through some other. If they didn't believe in his vision for the family, for the Syndicate, Dante could have them.

"Revoke his permissions and make sure everyone knows he's no longer with the Vitale family."

"Already done," Luca said.

"Good." Nico turned to face them. "There are over three hundred pages of search results from the piece of paper Angel found in her father's office, plus the data from John's computer. I suggest we get to work."

31

It was light out when she finally woke up, and she guessed that it was early morning from the weakness of the sunlight filtering into the room. She had a few precious seconds of peace before she remembered.

David. Her beautiful, gentle David. Hurt and disfigured by the animal that was Dante.

She moaned out loud, turned over in the empty bed, buried her face in the pillow as the tears came. There was no room for thought. There was only grief and fear. Sobs wracked her body, and she used the pillow to muffle the sound, heaving it out until could hardly draw breath.

The fact that David was out of reach to her, that he was hurting and probably scared and there wasn't a fucking thing she could do about it, emptied her out. Her chest constricted painfully. She wouldn't have been surprised if she stopped breathing. If her body simply gave up the fight. It hurt too much to keep living. How did people stand it?

But then she thought of David. Already it had been somewhere around twelve hours since she'd found the horrific message from Dante. She didn't know what Dante would do next, but David wasn't dead yet. He was out there, and she was his only hope for survival.

How far would you go to protect the ones you love?

She sat up in bed, shame washing over her as Luca's words rang through her mind. She had been so unforgiving of Nico, but she understood now why he'd pulled the trigger in London. If she were facing someone with a gun to David's head — or to Nico's — she wouldn't gamble their lives by hoping for the best. She would do what was necessary to insure their survival. And she would do it at any cost.

The pressure on her heart gave a little with the realization— she could breathe now at least — and she walked to the bathroom and splashed cold water on her face, then stared into the mirror.

"Who are you?" she asked the reflection quietly.

The question was met with silence, and she toweled off her face and headed for the kitchen. They were there — Sara, Luca, Marco, Elia, and of course, Nico. They looked up as she entered the room, and she took in the exhaustion on their faces, the cups of coffee and half-eaten sandwiches, the open computers and pieces of paper spread out on the table. They'd obviously been up all night working, digging through the data, hoping to find something that might lead them to David.

Nico crossed the room, put an arm around her, kissed her forehead. "How are you feeling?"

She looked up at him, then turned to the others. "I'm ready to find my brother now."

32

"This guy's a piece of work," Sara murmured, staring at her computer screen.

Angel looked up from the papers spread out in front of her. "Tell me you didn't need a background check to tell you that."

She and Sara had been working outside on the patio all day; Sara digging through Dante's history, hoping for a connection to LA, and Angel going through the data from John's computer piece by piece hoping for the same thing. Marco and Elia were inside, reviewing the security footage from storefronts near Ripley's. Nico was hoping they would catch sight of someone they recognized from the LA family, someone they could shake down for information about Dante's whereabouts.

Sara pulled her hair into a loose ponytail. "I mean, I knew something was... off about him."

Angel choked out a laugh. "Off?"

Sara sighed. "Okay, he scared me a little. But look at Marco and Elia. Look at Luca and Nico."

"What about them?" Angel leaned back in her chair and turned her eyes to Sara, grateful for a chance to look at something besides words on paper.

"Well... they can be scary. All the guys in the family can," Sara said. "It's hard to know who's good-scary and who's bad-scary, you know?"

She was right; to anyone outside of the family, Luca and Nico would be fearsome. They'd even been fearsome to her once. It was hard to believe now that she knew them. They were dangerous, yes. Even violent. But they had honor, and they only deployed violence when the situation called for it.

The train of thought took her by surprise. Was she rationalizing their criminal activity now? Making excuses for them? She didn't know, but everything looked a little different with David in danger.

"I guess I see what you mean," Angel said, taking a deep breath. "Dante... well, he tried to rape me once. Last year, before... everything."

Sara's eyes got wide. "Are you serious?"

Angel nodded, glad Luca had gone inside to call New York while Nico went to town for pizza. After her father's death, she'd had to be careful about what she said to Lauren, to everyone. It had been awhile since she'd been able to talk openly with a girlfriend.

"He and Luca were keeping an eye on me while Nico tried to get my father to come out of hiding."

"Luca didn't sanction it?" Sara said, her face pale.

"God, no!" Angel said. "He was the only person who made me feel safe, and he kept Dante in line when he was around. But one night, he wasn't, and Dante..." She shrugged, not wanting to remember what Dante was capable of while he had her brother.

"What happened?" Sara asked.

"I lied," Angel said. "Told him Nico wouldn't like it if he touched me."

"That's an understatement. I'm surprised he left Dante with any fingers." She winced. "Sorry."

"It's okay," Angel said, the horror of situation threatening to creep back in, to overshadow the tiny piece of calm she'd managed to claim while she was working. "It is what it is. I'm just glad David's alive."

Sara nodded. "And if anyone can keep him that way, it's Nico and Luca and the others."

Angel offered Sara the first smile she'd been able to muster all day. "I think you might be right."

A commotion broke out inside the house. They glanced at each other, then hurried inside to find Elia pacing the floor of Locke's living room, a blurry image frozen on the giant TV.

"Motherfucking coward!" he shouted.

"What's going on?" Luca asked, rushing into the room.

"Vincent Fucking Adamo, that's what's going on," Marco said.

Luca walked to the TV screen, peered at the grainy image.

Elia kept ranting. "That cocksucking, dog-fucking - "

"Hey." Luca stopped Elia in his tracks. "That's enough. The boss doesn't like that kind of talk in front of the ladies."

Elia looked sufficiently chastised. "Sorry."

Luca sighed. "This isn't a surprise. We suspected he was working with Dante. Unfortunately, he's not from the west coast, so it doesn't help us in terms of finding them. Keep looking. See if anyone else was there around the time Angel was in the museum."

She was on her way back to the patio when her cell phone rang from an unknown number. Luca signaled for everyone to be quiet, and she connected the call.

"Hello."

"How did you like your present?" Dante said on the other end of the phone. He sounded pleased with himself, and Angel had to fight the urge to unleash a string of obscenities that would rival the ones spoken by Elia.

"Please don't hurt David anymore," she said. "I'm... I'm working on what you want. I just need a little more time."

"I've got all the time in the world," he said. "But your brother..."

Tears stung her eyes. She blinked hard, forcing them away, and steadied her voice. "I'm going to get you what you want, Dante. I am. But I need a show of good faith, because right now, I'm not sure that you plan to hold up your end of the bargain."

"Do you think I care what you want, cunt?" he shouted.

Sara flinched, and Angel knew everyone in the room had overheard Dante's words.

"No, but you should," Angel said. "Because I'm the only one who can get you what you want, and I'm not going to do that if you hurt my brother."

"Don't flatter yourself," Dante said, his voice low and dangerous. "I have enough men who are sick of Vitale's pansy-ass policies to take New York by force. I'm just doing it this way out of respect for Donati."

"Raneiro?" Angel asked, dread knotting her stomach. "Does he know about this?"

"I think that's above your pay grade," Dante said. "Let's just say that I'm trying to play by the rules — rules Vitale made when he kidnapped you last year to get what he wanted. I suggest you do the same."

"That's the plan," Angel said. "But I need a show of good faith."

Silence descended on the other end of the phone, and for a minute, Angel thought he might have hung up. When he finally spoke, his voice was flat and hard.

"Seventy-two hours," he said. "Then you get more pieces of your brother."

33

Nico sat in the park, watching a bunch of kids run around on the playground. It wasn't as quiet as a church, but it was surprisingly relaxing.

He couldn't remember the last time he'd been around children. It must have been a birthday party or wedding back before he met Angel. After London, he hadn't been as engaged with his men, and he realized for the first time that he'd left himself — and them — vulnerable with his absence.

His father would be disappointed. He'd taught Nico how to lead, had prided himself on making his men feel like family in the truest sense of the word. Nico hadn't taken up the mantle lightly, and his father's leadership had been the benchmark by which Nico measured his own success.

Had his father struggled to balance his love for Nico and his mother with loyalty to the family? Had he ever gotten distracted? Made a mistake because of that love? Nico would give anything for one more conversation with him, one more moment with his mother. For the first time, he was unsure what to do, his judgement clouded by his warring feelings of love for Angel and loyalty to the family.

A small battle ensued on the playground, and he watched as a little boy tried to take a sand bucket from a girl with blonde pigtails. She held on tight to the plastic handle, refusing to give it up even as her eyes filled with tears. It made him think of Angel, and he found himself smiling, wondering what their children would be like, if they would have her spirit, her green eyes, her beautiful soul.

But that was ridiculous. She didn't belong in his world, and he didn't belong anywhere else. David was in danger because she'd tried to help him. Nico wouldn't say goodbye until she and her brother were safe again. But he would say goodbye. It's how it had to be.

A man about his age was jogging up the path next to the park. He stopped in front of the bench and bent over, resting his hands on his knees as he tried to catch his breath. Finally, still panting, he gestured to the bench.

"Mind if I sit?"

"Feel free," Nico said, keeping his eyes on the playground.

The man sat at the other end of the bench, looking out over the park as his breath slowly returned to normal. They sat in silence for a full minute before the man Nico knew as Agent Braden Kane spoke.

"You understand that I can't help you if you don't help me," Kane said.

Nico didn't look at him. "I'm not offering full cooperation. I need a little help. I'm willing to give you a similar measure of help. Tit for tat, so to speak."

"Might not be enough," Agent Kane said.

"It will have to be," Nico said.

Kane sighed. "Your friend Santoro is off the grid."

"That's why I'm talking to you," Nico said.

"You have cyber experts. Hell, you took some of them from us."

"True, but it will take us longer to find what we need on our own, and I don't have that kind of time."

"What do you need?" Kane asked.

"Anything that will lead us to Santoro. He's not using his own credit cards or bank accounts, but he's funding his operation somehow. Anything leading back to him would help, or even the location of known associates out here."

Kane got up, started stretching near the bench. Nico wondered if the FBI agent was really trying to squeeze in a workout or if it was all part of the act. It's not how Nico usually did business. He conducted meetings on his terms, in a suit. But this wasn't something he ever thought he'd do, and he still wasn't sure how far he was willing to take it. Kane had contacted him years ago, right after his father's death. They'd always been friendly, but Nico had made it clear that he had nothing to say. Calling him now was grounds for execution, and the meeting had been carefully set up so that no one but Nico would be implicated if Raneiro found out.

"What about Lando?" Kane asked.

There was no way Nico would confess to hacking John's computer. It was a federal offense, and he had no promise of immunity.

"He's not exactly a font of information," he said drily.

"I might be able to put out a few feelers," Kane said. "What are you offering in return?"

Nico combed the playground for the little girl. She was gone. He hoped she'd been able to keep her sand pail.

"William Molten lives in the Bronx," he said to Kane. "Had a pretty big kiddy porn ring going last year. He was trying to keep it a secret, run it through the family, but as you know, that's not something we allow."

"Is he still alive?" Kane asked.

"Yes," Nico said, "but only because I let him off with a warning. We've been keeping an eye on him, and I'm sorry to say, Bill hasn't entirely rehabilitated."

Kane nodded. "I'll look into it."

"And the other thing?" Nico asked.

"I'll look into that, too." He turned, preparing to pick up his run.

"Make it quick, Kane," Nico said softly. "I'm running out of time."

34

Angel sat next to Nico on the beach, their feet side by side in the sand. The moon hung wide and full over the water, scattering the sea with diamonds. Elia and Marco were wrestling at the break line. Farther out, Sara and Luca swam side by side. Angel was almost positive something was going on between them, but she wasn't sure she knew Sara well enough to ask about it.

She rested her head on her bent knees and looked at Nico. He was gazing out over the water, but his forehead was creased with worry, his eyes shaded with something she couldn't name. He'd been tense since coming home with the pizza, although it was possible she'd been too wrapped up in her own suffering to notice it before that. They were all tense — stressed out and exhausted from hours spent staring at security tapes or printouts or computer screens, all of them wracking their brains for a clue about Dante's whereabouts. She was glad to hear playful shouting from the water, glad the others were able to let off some steam. It would do them good.

"You okay?" she asked Nico.

He turned his eyes on her, and she felt the potent combination of love and lust that was a hallmark of her feelings for him.

"I'm fine." His voice was steady, his eyes clear. He took her hand, squeezed. "Don't worry about me."

"I do, though," she said.

"Don't," he repeated firmly. "I'm here to take care of you."

She knew how much it meant to him to be able to protect her, had seen the fury and frustration on his face when she'd told him about Dante's latest phone call.

She smiled a little. "It can go both ways, you know."

He took a drink of his beer. "Not for me."

She was about to argue the point when his phone rang from inside his jacket pocket. He scowled at the screen and walked a few feet away.

"Neiro. How are you?"

Angel sat up straighter. Raneiro Donati was calling Nico?

She didn't know a lot about Nico's relationship with the leader of the Syndicate, but she'd put enough of the pieces together to know that Nico respected him, cared for him like a father. A wall had dropped over Nico's face when she'd told him what Dante had said on the phone about "negotiating" for the New York territory out of respect for Raneiro, but not before she'd seen the look of confusion on his face.

"Yes," Nico said into the phone. "I'm working on it."

A pause filled only with the sound of waves rushing the beach, the soft murmur of conversation between Luca and Sara in the water.

"Of course. I'll meet you." Another pause. "I know. See you then."

He turned toward the house, his broad back to her, and she knew he was trying to gather his thoughts. She returned her gaze to the water. She could wait.

A couple minutes later, he dropped next to her in the sand.

"Everything okay?" she asked.

"Raneiro wants to meet," he said. "Tomorrow."

She looked at him. "He's here?"

"In the flesh."

"What do you think he wants?" Angel asked.

"I think he wants to tell me to get my shit together."

She reached for his hand. "Could he help us?"

"He could," Nico said. "But he won't."

"Why?"

He laughed, but there was no humor in it. "Because this is my punishment."

She shook her head. "Punishment? For what?"

He looked at her. "For going rogue when I took you last year."

"But… that was different." She couldn't believe she was saying it, but it was true. "My father…" She took a deep breath. "My father murdered your parents. You said that was against the Syndicate's code of honor."

"And it was," Nico said. "But by taking you, I only perpetuated the breaking of that code. I rewrote the rules, and now I have to play by them. That's what Raneiro wants me to know."

Angel looked away. "That's crazy."

He touched her cheek, made her look at him. "It's not, Angel. This is how it works. Every decision has a consequence. This is mine. I'm just sorry you have to suffer twice for my mistakes."

Their faces were close, his breath a whisper against her mouth. She touched her lips to his and slid her hand down his thigh, resting it against the rigid press of his erection. She wasn't surprised that he was hard. She only had to be near him and she was wet.

Ready for his cock, his fingers, his mouth.

She reached inside his pants, took the smooth length of him in her hand. She heard his breath catch in his throat.

"Let's go inside," she said.

He would take care of her, just like he said. But she would take care of him, too, even if it was only by making him forget for a little while.

35

Angel was working at the dining room table, the patio doors open to let in the sea breeze, when Nico bent to kiss her head.

"Morning," he said, heading for the coffee pot. "How long have you been up?"

"Couple of hours," Angel murmured, turning her attention from the stack of paper in front of her to the open laptop. Something was nagging at her in John's data, but she was still trying to figure it out.

"Where's everyone else?" he asked, returning to the table.

"Sara's working in her bedroom, Luca's making calls to the east coast, and the guys are shaking down some people they know out here for information."

He sat next to her and raised an eyebrow. "Shaking down, huh?"

She shrugged. "Their words."

"You should have woken me," he said. "We have a lot to do."

"Well, in the words of a very wise person I once knew, 'you're not good to anyone dead on your feet.'"

"Sounds like an asshole," Nico said.

She glanced up at him, forcing her eyes away from the words that were starting to blur in front of her eyes. He was shirtless, his defined abs pointing to a trail of dark hair that disappeared into sweats hanging low on his waist. He was a little rumpled, his dark hair messy, eyes hooded the way they were when he wanted to take her to bed.

"I kind of like him actually."

He reached for her hand. "Yeah?"

"Yeah."

She turned her attention back to the work in front of her.

"Find something?" Nico asked, taking a drink of his coffee.

"I'm not sure," she said. "I'm still figuring it out."

She didn't want to distract Nico from all the other angles he was working. There was a lot of data, and even though her brain told her she was missing something, she didn't entirely trust herself. She was too desperate. She wanted to find David too badly, and she was running mostly on coffee and take out. She wasn't exactly firing on all cylinders.

"Can I help?"

"Not yet. I'll let you know."

"Sounds good." He stood. "I'm going to shower."

"What time are we meeting Raneiro?" she asked.

He sighed. "Angel…"

She got up from her chair, wrapped her arms around his neck. She felt him soften against her and thrilled at the knowledge that she had the power to move so hard a man. That she was the one chink in his significant armor. But it scared her, too. She wanted him alive, and she'd learned the hard way that love was the greatest weakness of all.

"Let's not do this," she said. "My brother's life is at stake. And I think we both know that Raneiro is aware you and I are here together."

"That doesn't mean I want you exposed to him," he said.

"What difference does it make? I'm part of the Rossi family. Technically, the Boston organization is mine."

"That's temporary," Nico said. "Raneiro won't let Frank run things forever. He'll have the Syndicate appoint someone else soon enough."

"I understand, and I have no problem with that. But right now, I'm in it, and I'd rather know what I'm dealing with." He hesitated, and she took advantage of the moment to continue making her argument. "Besides, do you really think he doesn't know what I look like? How to find me? He probably knows more about me than I know about myself. Meeting him is just a formality, but it will make me feel better."

It took him awhile to answer. "I'll allow it."

"You'll allow it?"

He nodded. "That's right."

"You do know you're not the boss of me, right?" she asked him.

"I am right now." His voice had turned to cold steel. "If you don't like it, you can go back to New York and wait. Otherwise, you'll do as I say, like you agreed when we left Miami."

She wanted to argue on principle, but he was right; she'd agreed to his terms. And he had said she could go anyway. Why was she preparing to dig in her heels?

"I'll stay," she said, attempting to make her voice conciliatory instead of petulant. "And I'll do as you say. For now."

36

They arrived at the aquarium ten minutes early. Nico bought the tickets, and they entered into a large brick and concrete plaza. At its center, a large whale sculpture jumped toward the cloudless sky. Locke's mysterious coastal eddy had disappeared. Angel hoped it was a good omen.

They passed through a red metal gate and headed for a two-story building faced with stucco and fronted with glass. Continuing through a cavernous entry with full scale shark models hanging overhead, they followed the signs pointing to the Hall of Fishes and entered a warren of narrow hallways lined with water-filled tanks.

"Where are we meeting him?" Angel asked quietly.

"He'll find us," Nico said.

They continued through the labyrinthine exhibit, stopping to look at sea anemones, coral reefs, even kelp. It was quiet, the soft hum of the aquarium's filters the only sound emanating from the strangely muffled environment. It was like being in a submarine, the tanks portals to a watery world beyond the beige carpet and pale blue walls.

They had rounded yet another corner, Angel more disoriented than ever, when she saw the man staring at a tank full of electric eels. His dark hair was combed back from his face, and even in profile Angel could see that he had exquisite bone structure, with pronounced cheekbones and an aquiline nose that made her think of the sculptures she'd seen of Greek and Roman gods. He had the trim figure of someone in his twenties. His suit was well cut, obviously expensive.

Nico led the way, stopping when they reached the man and turning to look into the tank without speaking. Was there some kind of protocol to their meeting? Some reason they weren't supposed to greet Raneiro Donati? Angel didn't know, so she stood next to Nico in silence and followed his lead.

After a long moment, Raneiro spoke. "You brought the girl."

"My name is Angelica Rossi," she said. "But you probably know that."

She felt Nico tighten beside her.

"Of course."

He turned to face them, giving her a little bow. She didn't know what she expected. A thug in a leather jacket? A gun-toting Guido with more brawn than brains? Whatever it was, it hadn't been this; an obviously refined man with the manners of a king and the eyes of a cold-blooded killer.

He took her hand, brushed his lips against the back of it. "It's a pleasure to finally meet you. And now I see why you have caused so much trouble."

She didn't know whether to thank him or tell him to go fuck himself.

"This isn't her fault," Nico said.

The words were apologetic, but there was nothing remorseful in Nico's tone of voice. It had taken on the low, dangerous tone he used when he was issuing a warning. The baring of teeth before the bite.

"She is here," Raneiro said simply.

"Because Santoro has her brother," Nico said.

"Dante Santoro has her brother because of the changes you implemented after your father's death. Change I cautioned you against, if I remember correctly. And I always do."

"I'm right here," Angel snapped. "You can address me directly." She looked at Nico. "Both of you."

A faint smile touched Raneiro's lips. "Let's walk, shall we?"

It wasn't a request, and they fell into step beside him, winding their way through the exhibit as he continued speaking.

"I came to your aid last year, Nico, because I love you like a son. You know that don't you?"

"I do," Nico said.

"I'm sure you also remember my parting words; a caution that once the business with Carlo was finished, so too would be my involvement."

"Yes."

"Of course," Raneiro said, clasping his hands behind his back as they walked, "I assumed there would be no discord after the confrontation in London. I pulled strings to keep it quiet, you went back to New York, and Miss Rossi returned to her old life in…" he glanced over at her, "New Paltz is it?"

A trickle of ice water ran down her spine. She had been right; Raneiro had known where she was all along. And David, too, probably.

"That's right," she said. No point being coy about something he already knew.

He nodded, returned his gaze to the path in front of them. "And yet, here we are."

"Santoro could have left it alone," Nico said. "He didn't."

They emerged from the dimly lit hall onto an expansive patio. A nearby sign read TIDE POOL PLAZA. A metal railing separated the top of the terrace where they stood from a mini-lagoon enclosed by stone. A crowd of children bent over the pool of water, asking questions of a uniformed tour guide. Beyond them, the Pacific stretched blue-gray to the horizon.

"Dante isn't working alone," Raneiro said. "But I think you know that."

"I do," Nico said.

"Then you also know that Dante isn't alone in his view that your vision for the family doesn't honor its tradition."

"I'm not interested in what Dante Santoro thinks."

Nico's voice was weighted with lead, and Angel was suddenly afraid. This was not the exchange of mentor and student, loving father and son. The conversation was loaded with meaning, heavy with an unspoken threat Angel couldn't begin to understand.

"That's all well and good," Raneiro said. "But are you interested in what I think?"

"Of course, Neiro." Nico sighed. "Of course."

Raneiro leaned on the railing, every line of his body whispering elegance as he stared out to sea. "If this were simply one man standing in disagreement, Nico, I would call it defiance. Instead it's begun to look like a revolution."

"More like a devolution," Nico said.

"And you were the impetus of that devolution," Raneiro said sharply, straightening to look at them.

"That title belongs to Carlo," Nico said.

Raneiro's eyes skidded to Angel.

"I know what my father was," she said.

He nodded. "We will need to talk about the Boston family soon, although I realize now is not the best time." He returned his gaze to Nico. "I cannot stop this. It has the will of too many behind it."

"I understand," Nico said.

"But neither will I aid Dante Santoro at this time."

"Thank you," Nico said.

"However," Raneiro added, "my patience is not limitless, Nico. Even for you."

Nico nodded.

"I suggest you squash this rebellion, and soon, or I'm afraid it will not end well for you." He looked at Angel before returning his eyes to Nico. "Or for this beautiful creature next to you."

37

"How is it possible that you got nothing?"

Nico was trying to keep his voice even, but it got more and more difficult with every passing minute. They had forty-eight hours left on Dante's deadline, and the meeting with Raneiro hadn't exactly boosted his confidence. Angel had gone to the beach for a quick swim with Sara when they'd returned from the aquarium. Nico had stayed at the house to debrief with the men. Now he was wondering if there was any point.

Marco shrugged. "It's just…"

"What?" Nico prompted.

"Dead calm," Marco said. "You know?"

Nico did know. Dead calm was a sailing term for a weather condition in which everything at sea stopped — no wind, no current, nothing. He'd experienced it only once when he'd been out with his father after college. The sails had hung slack, the boat bobbing like a cork in a bathtub. They'd had to use the engine to get back to the harbor, something his father typically refused to do on principle.

"So no one's talking," Nico said.

"It's more than that, boss," Elia said. "It's like they're fucking *gone*."

"What does that mean?" It just wasn't possible for every mob contact Elia and Marco had on the west coast to disappear. "What about their families? Their businesses?"

"Everyone has a story," Marco said. "They're out of town for a wedding. They have a business meeting in San Francisco… But the gist of it is; they're all gone."

This was not good. This was an old-fashioned turf war, and soldiers were taking sides. Nico had been wrong; Dante didn't need to be smart to stage a coup. He just needed to be crazy enough to try and dynamic enough to get boots on the ground behind him — or convince the ones who wouldn't to stay out of the way until it was over. Something that obviously hadn't been very difficult. Nico remembered Raneiro's words at the aquarium that afternoon.

It's begun to look like a revolution.

Was it true? Did a majority of the soldiers want things to stay the same? Did they prefer brutality to civility?

The thought depressed him. He knew a majority of the men and women in New York supported his vision, but they weren't in New York anymore, and the one smart thing Dante had done was to stage his takeover from California where Nico's influence was significantly smaller.

"So someone put the word out," he said. "We'll find another way. How are we doing on the security footage?"

"Vincent is the only one we saw," Marco said.

"So back to square one there, too," Nico said as his phone rang. He looked at the display and glanced at Marco and Elia. "I have to take this in the other room. Keep working."

He headed for the bedroom he shared with Angel and shut the door, then went onto the balcony where the surf would cover his conversation.

"Kane."

"I've got something," Agent Kane said on the other end of the phone.

"Hit me."

"Santoro's got a big family, but they've all been steering clear of him publicly," Kane said.

"That's not new information," Nico said. "Santoro's father used to work for my father. I sent some men to try and shake him down after Santoro escaped in London, and again when it became clear my operations were being targeted. Said he hadn't talked to Dante since last October, right before the shit hit the fan."

"Right, but here's the thing," Kane said. "Santoro has a great-aunt that's really old — I'm talking infirm and in a home — and that great-aunt recently wired a large sum of money to a bank in…" Nico heard the tap of computer keys in the background as Kane hunted for the information, "Redondo Beach, California."

That got his attention. "Redondo Beach?"

"Yep," Kane said. "Mean anything to you?"

Nico weighed his words. "I don't know yet. What's the name of the bank?"

"First National on PCH and 190th." Kane hesitated. "You know I can't cover for you if you do something stupid, right?"

"I know. Was there anything else on Santoro?"

"He's completely dark," the FBI agent said. "No credit cards, no rental cars, no hotel rooms. He's obviously getting help from someone, and I'm betting it's not old Aunt Mary. "

Nico was betting the same thing. "Did you get Molton?"

"Brought him in this morning," Kane said. "You were right. His computer was loaded with some really nasty shit."

"Enough to put him away?"

"For a long time," Kane confirmed.

"Good."

"Thanks for that, Vitale. And if you change your mind about cooperating, you know where to find me."

"I won't," Nico said. "But I appreciate the help with this one."

He disconnected the call and leaned against the balcony's railing, fighting the guilt that crept into his veins. He was officially a traitor to the Syndicate. He may have given up an ex-member, and a despicable one at that, but that's not how they did things. Violators of the family's code were dealt with privately, albeit sometimes brutally. Giving a member up to the Feds was the equivalent of high treason.

A year ago, Nico could have held firm in his belief that anyone betraying the family's code of silence be executed as a message to others. But a lot of things had been different a year ago. Most importantly, he hadn't known Angel. Hadn't known what it meant to love the way he loved her.

It shouldn't matter. Conviction was only conviction if you were willing to stand by it in the most trying of times, and Nico had always prided himself on being the kind of man who was.

Now he found that it did matter, and he couldn't help wondering if the end really did justify the means. Violating the Syndicate's honor code seemed like a small price to pay to save the life of David Rossi.

Would he have felt that way if David wasn't Angel's brother? Nico wanted to believe he would bend the rules to save any innocent, but the truth was that Angel short-circuited his previously reliable pragmatism. He thought of her soft body, the green eyes that could see into his soul, the heart that was both gentle and fierce, and knew he would do anything — anything — to protect her.

A soft knock on the door interrupted his thoughts, and he turned away from the balcony and headed back into the bedroom.

"Come in."

Luca opened the door. "You busy?"

"It's fine," Nico said.

Luca entered the room. "Just got off the phone with New York."

"Anything new?"

Luca shook his head. "It's business as usual. No more theft, no more beatings. Now that Dante is negotiating directly with you — or with you through Angel — it seems like they've laid off the operation. Probably wants to keep it intact for himself," Luca growled.

"That's fine," Nico said, fortifying his resolve. "Let him think he has a chance. I don't want the men harassed while they're going about their business."

"Anything new on your end?" Luca asked.

Nico told him about the wire transfer from Dante's great-aunt.

Luca raised an eyebrow. "Redondo Beach?"

Nico nodded.

"The South Bay…."

"That's right," Nico said.

"And you know this how?" Luca asked.

Nico crossed his arms over his chest. He wasn't going to implicate Luca in his communication with the FBI. "Not important."

Luca nodded his understanding. "So he has to be in the South Bay."

"The few clues we have all seem to point in that direction."

Luca rubbed the stubble on his cheek. He looked tired and worn out. Nico wondered how long it had been since his Underboss had taken a break.

"What do we do now?"

"I don't know," Nico said, clapping him on the back. "But I think it's time for a change of scenery."

38

They went to a little bar near the beach. Angel didn't want to go, didn't want to leave the search results and reports that had started to feel like an extension of her brain. But Nico insisted, saying that everyone was exhausted and worried, and no one worked well under that kind of pressure. When Angel told him they could go without her, he'd told her no one else would feel right going if she didn't come along. It was a little underhanded, but now that they were sitting in the beach-themed bar, the Pacific rushing the sand beyond a patio surrounded by tiki torches, she knew he'd had been right. She needed this. Needed to clear her head to make sense of all the names, dates, and locations swirling around inside of it.

"Feeling better?" he asked, setting another mysterious umbrella drink in front of her.

"I do, actually." She pushed the drink toward him. "But not good enough to drink another one of those."

"I thought you could hold your liquor," he said.

"And I thought you said one drink."

He grinned. "Touché."

Her heart skipped a beat. His animalistic grace made him as sexy in the faded jeans and black button-down as he looked in any of his five-thousand dollar suits. His hair was a little longer than usual — probably because he'd been too preoccupied finding David to maintain his customary tailored appearance — and his skin had darkened slightly from the time spent on Locke's patio and at the beach below the house.

Angel's eyes strayed to Sara and Luca, playing pool with Marco and Elia inside the bar.

"Think something's up with those two?" Angel asked.

"Marco and Elia?"

Angel laughed a little, shaking her head. "Very funny. Sara and Luca."

Nico's expression darkened. "Probably."

"Would that be a bad thing?" Angel asked.

He took a swig of his beer. "Probably."

"Why?"

"Because mixing business and pleasure is a dangerous proposition," he said, his eyes on the foursome. "Especially in our business."

Angel followed his gaze, watched Sara sink the ten ball into a side pocket on a bank shot. "But Sara's not in the field, right?"

"Sara has enough information to sink our whole operation," Nico said. "That makes her more valuable as an asset than most of the men who work for me."

"An asset? Is that how you think of her?"

"Of course not," Nico said. "But that's how someone else might think of her. There's no reason to give anyone added incentive to have an eye on her. That's all I'm saying."

"You mean someone might target her because of Luca?" The idea sent a clang of alarm through Angel's body. She knew Sara was ridiculously smart, talented enough that she'd once been in training for the FBI. But she was also nice and genuine. Angel didn't want to think about her in the hands of someone who might see her as a way to get to the Vitale family.

Nico leveled his amber eyes at her. "They targeted you, didn't they?"

She took a sip of the drink in front of her, forgetting her earlier resolve to quit while she was ahead. She wouldn't think about Sara and Luca right now. They were fine. It was David who needed her help, and they had less than forty-eight hours to do it. She needed to focus, compartmentalize. She was on overload, the alcohol barely keeping her panic at bay.

"Please tell me we're getting closer," she said, unable to keep the fear out of her voice.

Nico took her hand. "We're getting closer."

"Are you just saying that to make me feel better?" she asked.

"No. I got some information today. I'm just not sure how it fits with everything else we know."

Hope sprang to life inside her. "Tell me."

"Someone wired money to Dante here in California. In Redondo Beach, to be exact."

She sat up straighter, her mind clearing. "Redondo Beach… That's in the South Bay."

"It is," Nico said. "We're still trying to figure out who sent it, but it looks like it came from his family."

"Where?" she asked softly, her mind beginning to turn.

Nico looked confused. "Where is his family?"

"Where did they wire the money?"

"A bank," he said. "On PCH and 190th."

She turned her face toward the water, let the salty breeze kiss her face. Something was there… something from the data on John's computer…

"What is it?" Nico asked.

PCH and 190th… an intersection at the crossroads of three towns in the South Bay.

She stood so fast her chair fell to the floor behind her. "We need to get back to the house. Now."

He looked at her for a long moment before going inside to round up the others. She loved him for that. For the fact that he hadn't asked any more questions. That he trusted her and believed in her.

Her mind worked all the way home, Nico driving her in the Porsche while Luca and the others followed in one of Locke's SUVs. She watched their headlights in the side mirror, but she wasn't really seeing them. She was seeing the map she'd left open on Locke's computer, the intersection of PCH and 190th, the neighboring beach towns stacked with houses and apartment buildings and condos.

She was out of the car before Nico had turned off the engine. The house was dark, but she didn't bother with the lights. They came on behind her as Nico entered the house, following her to the laptop on the dining room table where she'd left it.

"Are you going to tell me what's going on?" he asked as Luca, Sara, Marco, and Elia came into the room.

She zoomed in on the map, then tabbed to a spreadsheet filled with company names and addresses.

"There's a property listed here..." she murmured, searching the list that had been extracted from Lando's computer. "There!" She pointed to an address owned by a company called Big Bear Holdings — a company owned by John Lando.

Nico leaned in to get a closer look. "2041 Strand, Hermosa Beach."

Angel opened a new tab and typed in an address. An almost real-time aerial image opened up, a strip of concrete running in front of a big yellow house surrounded by other houses.

She tabbed back to the map, zooming in even closer until they were looking at the Strand. It wasn't a street exactly, but a concrete walkway used by runners and skaters near the water. And one of the most expensive addresses in Southern California.

"2041 is here," she said, pointing to Hermosa Beach on the map.

"And?" Nico prodded.

She zoomed out just a little, then ran her finger a short distance from the house to a street corner. "And PCH and 190th is here. Less than half a mile away."

39

Nico spent most of the next day deep in conversation with the men while Angel paced the house.

"This is ridiculous," she said to Sara when her frustration got the best of her. "They act like it's the 1950s. Like we're too fragile to be involved or something!"

"I know it seems that way," Sara said, "but it's not about that."

"Then what is it?" Angel seethed. "My brother's life is at stake. I think I have a right to know what's going on."

"You do," Sara said. "And you will. But Nico doesn't want to run you around with a bunch of possibilities. He's going to figure out the pieces, get a plan in place to save your brother. Then he'll tell you about it."

"I don't see what difference it makes," Angel said.

"These guys know how to stage the kind of operation that will get your brother out alive. It will be better for David if you let them figure it out. They'll fill you in as soon as they have a plan."

Angel had grudgingly kept quiet after that, her stomach doing somersaults while the hours ticked by. She and Sara were starting dinner, the sun hanging low over the water, when Luca finally stepped into the room. Sara's eyes slid to his for a split second before she returned her gaze to the Bolognese simmering on the stove. A moment later the intercom buzzed.

Luca walked to the security display, then spoke briefly in Italian before pressing the button to open the gate. Angel hadn't realized he spoke the language when they'd been in Rome last year, although it made sense. Nico spoke it, too.

"Mattia and Aldo," he explained as he headed for the front door.

Were the names supposed to make some kind of sense to her?

She heard voices coming from the entry, and a couple minutes later, Luca returned with two dark-eyed men. Introductions were made — Mattia had the soft features of someone half his size, while Aldo was lean and quiet, his face as unreadable as stone — and a few minutes later, Nico and the other men emerged from Locke's office.

Angel wanted to know what was going on — they had less than twenty-four hours to get her brother out before Dante's deadline — but Nico insisted on sitting everyone down, pouring wine, having dinner. She was beginning to recognize it as a hallmark of Vitale family hospitality — food and wine before business, no matter how important that business may be, with at least a little time for conversation.

Mattia and Aldo were every bit as big as Elia and Marco, although not nearly as talkative. When they did speak, it was with a thick accent. Were they members of the New York family? Or had they been brought in from Italy specifically to help free David? And how could everyone eat and talk like something horrible wasn't about to happen when Angel had such a terrible feeling about the next twenty-four hours?

She sat next to Nico, watching the men shovel pasta with Sara's Bolognese sauce into their mouths between healthy drinks of the merlot Luca brought up from Locke's wine cellar. Her stomach was in knots, and she could only pick at her food as the new arrivals regaled the other with tales from the New York family.

It's not that she begrudged them their enjoyment. Not everyone should live in self-imposed misery because of what was happening with her brother. But it was still hard to realize that for everyone else, this was a mission, a business related operation — not the life or death scenario it was for Angel and her brother.

And it was life or death for them both, because she wasn't sure she could go on without him. He was all the family she had left.

She glanced at Nico and felt a pang of regret. She wasn't giving him enough credit. It was more than business for him, too. She could see it in the shadows under his eyes, the tired set of his jaw. Luca and Sara looked worried, too. In fact, a closer glance around the table revealed signs of stress in everyone — Marco's forced laughter, Elia's quiet rage, even Mattia and Aldo's somberness could have been a sign of their concern.

They cared. She could see it now. Could feel it. They were just doing what people had always done when faced with an uncertain outcome — taking their laughter and love where they found it, tasting life while they could. It was a sign of their humanity, just as her all-encompassing fear was a sign of her own.

Finally, when the pasta was gone and the wine bottles emptied, Nico pushed back from the table.

"Let's go into the other room."

Angel stood. She'd been patient, had let them plan their way. Now she needed to know how they were going to save her brother.

She exhaled her relief as he took her hand and led her to the living room. He wouldn't fight her after all.

Nico cleared the coffee table and unrolled a map while everyone got settled. The Pacific was clearly visible along one side of the map, a densely packed neighborhood of houses stretching in every direction on the other. Angel knew immediately that it was a map of the neighborhood where they suspected Dante was holding David.

Nico used some of Locke's books to hold down the edges, then stood back.

"You all have an encrypted copy of this map in your secure email, but it's easier to talk about as a group this way." He used a red Sharpie to make a circle around one of the houses on the map. "This is where Dante is holding David Rossi."

"Bondesan," Angel corrected him. David wouldn't want to be associated with their dead father that way. "And how do we know for sure?"

She knew the conclusion was probable, but she didn't want to waste time and effort planning a siege only to crash in on some surfer smoking a joint in his living room.

"Mattia and Aldo cased the place on their way down from the airport," Nico said.

Angel sat up straighter. "They saw David?"

"Not exactly," Nico said. "But they saw Dante, and I think it's safe to say that he's sticking close to David."

"But we don't know?" She had to have all the information, even if it meant being scared. Even if it meant knowing they might not succeed.

"We know with as much certainty as we can, given the time we have left," Nico said.

There was regret in his voice, but he was telling her the truth. That was all she could ask for at this point. She nodded.

"There are three doors," he marked the front and rear entrances, plus a set of doors leading to a second floor balcony. "Unfortunately, there are also lots of windows. Those are secondary concerns. Dante's men might escape that way, but Dante will try to get David out through one of the conventional exits. Angel's brother is the only negotiating tool he has. He's going to try and keep him alive, especially once he realizes we've outed his operational headquarters."

"I'll get David out the back and bring him down this alley here." He pointed to a tiny strip of pavement at the back of the house.

"What about Sara and me?" Angel asked.

"You'll be right here," Nico said, his voice as cold as ice.

Angel crossed her arms. "Well, I can't speak for Sara, but I definitely won't be here. I'll be *there,* helping you get my brother out in one piece."

"No, you won't," he said through his teeth. "It will be a distraction. One we can't afford."

"You are all professionals," she said stubbornly. "I'm sure none of the men here will be distracted by my presence. You showed me how to use a gun. I can protect myself."

"You'll be a distraction to *me,*" he roared.

Everyone froze. Nico turned away from them, stalked to the liquor cabinet. He poured a drink and downed it in one swallow. When he turned around, his eyes were bright with anger.

"You've fired a gun exactly one time." He was looking at her, talking to her, like they were the only two people in the room.

"You told me it was so I could protect myself."

"And it is," he said. "But not in a dangerous situation that I put you in."

She saw the fear lurking behind his frustration, and her heart softened. "I have to be there, Nico. I *have* to."

The room was heavy with silence. Finally, Luca spoke.

"The house two addresses down is empty."

Nico glared at him.

"What do you mean?" Angel asked.

"It's a vacation rental," Luca explained. "It's empty right now."

"We could use the body cams," Elia said.

"I don't want her anywhere near that house," Nico said.

She should have been glad he was no longer shouting, but she knew from experience that sometimes the time to be most scared was when Nico lowered his voice. Luca and the others must have known it, too, because they shuffled a little on their feet, looked idly around the room like there was something fascinating on the walls, the floor, the sofa.

"If you let me watch," Angel said, "I won't feel like I have to go to the other house on my own."

She hated to reference London. Hated to remind him that the last time he'd excluded her, she'd gone ahead and shown up anyway. But she was so scared. She needed to be close to David when he was rescued, needed to know for herself that he would be okay.

Nico paced to the windows overlooking the courtyard out front and turned his back to them. For a long moment, no one said anything, and the only sound in the room was the faint crash of the surf against the rocks below the house. Finally, he turned around.

"Sara stays with you. And so help me, Angel, if you take it upon yourself to leave that house…"

"I won't."

She saw defeat in the slope of his shoulders and felt it like a stab to the heart. She didn't want to be a burden to him. Didn't want to make things harder than they already were. But this was her brother. He was her only remaining family, and he was her responsibility. She would be as much a pain in the ass as she had to be to make sure he made it out of this alive.

Nico looked at the others. "We leave at midnight."

40

He sat on the beach below the house, rolling the rosary beads between his fingers and thinking about his mother. She wouldn't call him a hypocrite for returning to the old habit in a time of trouble.

"That's what faith is, Nico," she would say. *"The one thing that never fails if you hold tight enough."*

It was true in a way, which wasn't to say it guaranteed a specific outcome. The rosary was still there after months away from it. The beads were smooth and cool in his hand, just like he remembered, the ritual as calming as the waves rushing toward his bare feet.

He looked out over the water. He couldn't see the moon, but somewhere high above the earth, it lit enough of the sky to cast shimmering light over the surface of the sea. He felt strangely detached from the activity going on inside the house — the gathering of weapons and cameras, the loading of ammunition. Soon enough they would be on their way north to the South Bay, the string of beaches west of Los Angeles where Dante had been holding David. Nico would have a chance to redeem himself by saving David, and he would see it done, even if the aftermath meant leaving Angel for good.

She would have her brother, her family. It was what he wanted for her.

He felt the eventual loss of her like an ever-widening hole in his heart. The family was no place for her, and he didn't delude himself into thinking saving David would change anything.

It would only be the beginning.

They would rescue Angel's brother, but his kidnapping was only a symptom of a much bigger problem. There were many in the family — and in the Syndicate as a whole — that didn't agree with Nico's vision. That was obvious now, and he'd been foolish to discount the dissenters as a powerless minority.

Everyone makes mistakes, Nico.

It was something his father had said Nico when Nico fucked up, when he'd beaten himself up over every misstep. And of course, his father had been right. Nico wasn't narcissistic enough to believe he was an exception. But acknowledging the mistake wasn't enough.

That was something his father had taught him as well.

Once David was safe, Nico would need to rectify the bigger problem, and that would make things even more dangerous for Angel.

Would removing Dante from the equation make her safer? Undoubtedly. She would go back to her quiet life, maybe move someplace new, start over with her brother. It was a gift he would give her by killing Dante once and for all. Then she would be free.

He rolled the rosary beads between his fingers, searching for the words he hadn't spoken in more than two years.

"Our father, who art in heaven…" he murmured.

Did he believe it? Fuck, he didn't know. But it was worth a shot.

41

Angel found him on the beach, speaking softly to himself while he stared out over the water. She approached him slowly, wondering if he was angry. She'd pushed him in front of the men, had undermined his authority. She wouldn't blame him if he was mad, but she couldn't let that stop her from being there for David.

"Hey," she said, dropping next to him on the sand.

"Hey." He didn't look at her, just kept staring out over the water.

She noticed his hand moving, and when she looked closer she saw that he was holding something in his palm, working it between his fingers. Mala beads? Unlikely. She thought of her own Catholic upbringing and realized he had been saying the rosary.

"Would you like me to leave you alone?" she asked.

He took her hand in his own. "No."

She followed his gaze across the water. "I'm sorry."

"I'm trying to protect you, Angel. That's all I'm ever trying to do."

"I understand that," she said. "But I need to be there for my brother, and I guess that means our goals aren't always aligned."

He turned to look at her, his panther eyes piercing hers through the darkness. "You don't trust me to save him."

She shook her head. "There's no one I trust more. I just…" She faltered, trying to find the words to explain.

"Continue," he prompted.

"I just need to be there," she said. "When you save him, I need to be there. And if something goes wrong…" She hardly dared to voice the fear. "I'll want to be there then, too."

"It's a mistake," he said stonily.

"Then it's my mistake," she snapped.

"You have no idea what you're doing," he said tightly.

"Just because you disagree with me, doesn't mean I'm wrong," she said.

"In this case, I'm afraid it does."

Anger swelled through her body. There were times when his Alpha male, domineering, know-it-all attitude was a turn on — but this was not one of them.

She stood, brushing the sand off her legs, bare under a long skirt. "Then I guess we'll just have to agree to disagree."

She headed for the path leading back to the house. She made it to the base of the staircase before she felt his hand on her arm. He spun her around, pinned her against a flat piece of rock that rose to the cliffs on Locke's property.

"I don't think you get it," he said, his voice ragged, face only inches from hers.

"Get what?" She had to force the question from her mouth, force her brain to formulate the words. She was back in Nico's orbit, struggling to maintain contact with the ground when the pull of his gaze, his hands, his body, threatened to set her loose in space.

He lowered his face to her neck, inhaling like an animal sniffing its prey, nuzzling the tender skin at her collarbone. "I can't think straight when you're around, Angel. Can't worry about anyone but you. Can't see anyone but you."

Her head fell to the side, giving Nico better access to the side of her neck as he moved closer, insinuating one thigh between her legs until it pressed against her warmth.

"I… I'm sorry," she said as he nipped at her ear, the heat of his breath sending a jolt of heat to her center.

"Sorry for what?" His voice was a growl. "For doing this to me?"

She gasped as he pressed his hard-on into her. Her belly tightened in response, and a swell of desire rolled through her.

"I don't know," she choked out as his hips ground into hers. She was nearing the point of no return; that familiar place with Nico where none of their differences mattered, where she couldn't think about anything but the feel of him driving into her.

"For making me so fucking crazy about you that I can't think straight?" he said, kissing his way across her cheek until he reached the corner of her mouth. "For making me want to walk away from everything but you?"

"I'm just sorry everything's so… hard," she said, trying to keep her focus on the conversation. Somewhere in the recesses of her mind, she knew it was important, but that part of her brain was so far away from the feel of Nico's mouth on her skin, his knuckles brushing her cheek on their way down her neck.

"Oh, it's hard alright," he said, sliding his hands down the side of her body.

She felt the heat of his palms on her legs as he moved his hands under her skirt, lifting it on his way back up her body. The cool ocean air brushed against her bare skin as the fabric bunched around her waist. Then he was lifting her off the ground, wrapping her legs around his waist as he pressed her against the rock. They were in a world of their own making, sheltered from the house above by the craggy cliffs, the moonless night.

He positioned himself so his cock was pressed into the "V" between her legs, and she gasped at the exquisite torture of it. He was so close, his erection only separated from her heat by his jeans and the thin satin of her underwear.

She grabbed his ass and pressed him harder into her. He groaned, his breath a whisper against her lips in the moment before he captured her mouth with his.

There was no build to the kiss. He dove into her mouth like he did everything else; devouring, occupying, owning. There was no half-measure with Nico, and definitely not with her. He took the kiss deep, pressing his whole body into hers as he tasted her. She met his passion with a ferociousness of her own, sinking her hands into the silky hair at the back of his head while he pulled down her tank top, freed her breasts from her bra.

The air hit her already sensitive nipples, and she moaned as he cupped her breasts, thumbing one of the nipples while he gently pinched the other one.

He pulled his mouth from hers and bent his head, closing his lips over one of the tiny buds. The heat of it against her cool skin was like a stone thrown at her center, the desire rippling outward in waves. She arched her back, offering herself to him as she pushed her hips against the length of his shaft through his jeans.

She moved one hand between them as he sucked, the feel of his tongue against her erect nipple like a match to a flame. Reaching for the top button of his jeans, she freed his cock, reveling at the smoothness of it, hard and heavy with his need for her.

"Fuck, Angel," he grunted, lifting his head to look at her. "You have no idea what you do to me."

"Show me," she said, stroking him, feeling him lengthen in her palm.

He lowered one hand between them and ripped away her underwear. Then he was right there, his cock hot and silky against the folds of her sex.

"Nico…" She pushed against him, seeking the connection, the moment when his head was poised at her entrance, the moment right afterwards when filled her.

"You want it?" He was grinding against her, his tip rubbing against her clit until she thought she might come before he ever entered her.

"Yes," she gasped. "Please."

"Please?" His voice low and laced with sex. "Don't get polite on me now, Angel."

She reached for him then, positioned him at her opening. "Shut up and fuck me, Nico."

He growled, then plunged his tongue into her mouth as he thrust into her.

He pulled almost all the way out and drove into her again, her cries snatched by the sound of the waves rushing up the beach, the crashing of water against the rocky cliffs.

He cupped her ass, spreading her wider while she locked her legs around his waist, forcing him deeper. Then he was moving fast and sure inside of her, letting her feel the length of him every time he withdrew, every time he pushed into her again.

She was moving with him now, rocking in time to the primal ebb and flow of the ocean moving up the beach, retreating back into the ocean, the sounds of it mingling with their passion until they were one with the primitive forces of nature.

She felt the orgasm like a primordial tug at the center of her body, felt Nico getting bigger and harder as she grew tighter around him, her muscles contracting in the build up to finally letting go, the moment when they would tumble into the abyss together.

He took her hands, raised them over her head, held them against the rock. She felt the cold stone against her skin in contrast to the heat of Nico's body against her own. She was stretched out, every inch of her body, every secret corner, open to him as he drove into her again and again.

"Oh, god," she gasped. "I can't…"

"Come for me, baby," he said. "Come for me."

She looked into his eyes. "You come for me, Nico."

He growled, thrusting into her with even more force until she came apart in his hands, tumbling over the precipice all at once, feeling him fall with her. She bit down on his shoulder, trying to muffle the cries she couldn't contain as she shuddered again and again around him, the orgasm going on and on. He didn't stop moving inside her until he'd wrung every last tremor from her body.

He slumped against her, his head falling against her shoulder while their breathing slowly returned to normal. Finally, he raised his head, looked into her eyes.

"I have to keep you safe, Angel," he said. "I have to."

42

They were on the road just after midnight; Angel, Nico, Luca, and Sara in one of the SUVs while Elia, Marco, Mattia, and Aldo followed in another. Angel watched Orange County pass on the other side of the window, lights casting pools of color across the pavement. Everything looked different at night. Darker, like the gloss had been rubbed off a shiny photograph. They pulled off the freeway in Hawthorne, then made their way west toward the beach.

She wanted to be excited. If all went well, she would be back together with David in just a few hours. But it was the "if all went well" part that scared her. There was a lot that had to happen between now and any moment when she had David back.

And a lot that could go wrong.

Nico's hand closed over hers across the console of the car. "You okay?"

She nodded. Already their moment on the beach seemed a lifetime away. She wanted to go back. To let Nico's body cover hers - the only time she really felt safe. But she couldn't hide behind Nico. Not now, and not after David was rescued. She would have to stand on her own two feet, and she wouldn't be able to do it beside Nico. Her responsibility was to David. And to keep David safe, she would have to distance herself from Nico.

It was after two am as they made their way toward Hermosa Beach, the streets nearly empty, other cars few and far between. The witching hour. Isn't that what they called it? It seemed strangely appropriate, and she wondered suddenly what it meant, where the figure of speech had come from.

She watched Locke's second SUV in the rearview mirror. They were all in it now, for better or worse. She felt the weight of it. All these people, trying to save her brother. Was this what it was like for Nico, day in and day out? Knowing that one mistake, one doomed operation, could cost his men — and women like Sara — their lives? How did he stand it?

She shook her head. She was being stupid. Nico and his men did what they did by choice. Sara, too. It wasn't the same as she and David becoming pawns in a greedy game of chess. She had always been honest with herself about Nico, about what he did and who he was. It hadn't stopped her from loving him, from wanting him, but she hadn't been a liar at least. She wouldn't start now.

The breeze coming in through the window changed as they got closer to the beach. It smelled like Locke's house, like sea and salt and moisture in the air. They must be close.

Nico turned right on the Esplanade and headed north. They traveled about a half a mile, past apartment buildings, hip sushi restaurants, and a pier that jutted out into the darkness, lights illuminating the water on either side. Finally, Nico turned into a tiny alley, checking in his mirror to make sure the other SUV was still following. They pulled into an empty carport, and Nico turned off the car.

"The house is farther down the Strand," he said. "I don't want to park too close. We'll gear up here."

They got out and moved to the back of the SUV. Elia, Marco, Aldo, and Mattia got out of the second car, parked alongside the carport. Dressed head to toe in black, the men looked like the criminals they were — either that or like the kind of men who took down criminals. Maybe both. She could tell from their easy movements that this wasn't the first time they'd been deployed on this kind of mission.

"Keep it down," Nico said softly. "It's late."

They nodded, and Nico opened the trunk. Angel had recognized the two duffel bags when the men loaded them up, but they didn't scare her now. She just hoped their contents did more good this time than they had at the museum.

Nico unzipped one of the bags and extracted a heavy duty laptop. He handed it to Sara, and she opened the computer in the back of the SUV and started tapping at the keys. While she worked, Nico passed out tiny headsets to the men. After they'd put them in their ears, Nico handed each man a black piece of plastic, which they all proceeded to clip to their shirts. A moment later, a grainy image appeared on the laptop.

"Got you," Sara said.

Angel peered over her shoulder. It took her a few seconds to orient herself to the image on the screen. Then she got it; she was looking at Nico's face and chest, projected from the camera clipped to Luca's shirt.

Sara hit a few more keys, and five more boxes appeared on the screen, each of them broadcasting from one of the body cams.

"All present and accounted for," she murmured, shutting the laptop.

"Good," Nico said, turning his attention to the second bag.

A mini-arsenal was inside — big, scary looking weapons that Angel thought must be semi-automatics from Locke's stash. Nico handed one gun to each of the men, then surprised Angel by handing one to Sara.

"She's as well trained as the men," Nico explained when he saw the expression on Angel's face.

She glanced at Sara, who just shrugged. She had never said she wasn't trained like the men who worked in the field. In fact, it made sense that she would be; Nico left nothing to chance. He wouldn't allow anyone on his team — male or female — who couldn't hold his or her own. Still, Angel felt strangely betrayed, like she'd just found out her best girlfriend was an undercover spy when the truth is, she didn't know Sara at all, and she was probably a lot closer to a spy than a garden variety computer geek.

Nico handed out extra ammunition, then finished by handing out wicked looking knives and night vision goggles. By the time he was done, Angel's nerves were strung tight. The show of force represented by the weapons gave her the feeling this wasn't going to be an easy mission. More like a full on assault.

"Obviously, we want to go in and get out as quietly and as quickly as possible," Nico said, looking at the others. "But the number one imperative is to get David Bondesan out alive. That will be my job, as we discussed. The rest of you lock down the house. Quietly. The houses are too fucking close together, and we don't have enough clout out here to keep it quiet like we could in New York."

"What about Santoro?" Luca asked.

His voice was too even. Angel was scared by the cold fury in it. It was like falling down the rabbit hole all over again; she was surrounded by men who were as chivalrous as they were deadly, who's capacity for violence was measured not by their lack of control, but by the measure of calm a situation forced them to exercise. A world where the time to be scared was not when one of them was mindless with anger, but when they were brought to quiet stillness by their rage.

"Santoro is mine," Nico said flatly. "And this time it will get done right."

She should have been shocked, even disgusted. She knew what Nico meant. Knew that this time, he would kill Dante. But she was surprised to find that she didn't care. The world would be better off without him.

People will show you who they are if you listen.

She heard her father's voice, registered with detachment the alteration in her character. It was entirely justified, she thought coldly. Nico would take care of Dante, and he would never hurt someone like he'd hurt David. She would think later about what it meant that she had come to this place. Right now all that mattered was getting David out alive.

Nico put the empty duffel bag in the trunk and handed the one with the laptop to Sara. Then he removed a key from his pocket and handed that to her as well.

"You know the address?"

She nodded.

"The house is empty, but keep the lights off in case a neighbor's watching." His gaze flickered to Angel. "And don't let her out of your sight."

He withdrew a pistol from the holster strapped to his body. "This is the same gun you fired at Locke's range," he said. "Remember; keep the safety on, and don't point it unless you mean to shoot."

She nodded, and he gave it to her handle first. She wrapped her hands around it without hesitation, grateful for the cold weight of it.

He looked at her for what seemed like too long given the circumstance, then slipped his hands into the hair at the back of her head, crushed his lips to hers.

"I'm going to get him out," he said. "But you stay put no matter what." He looked at the men. "Let's go."

They turned away and were swallowed by the night seconds later.

"Come on," Sara said softly. "We need to get into position, too."

43

The house was big but unremarkable, a stucco box with large windows that looked out over the strip of concrete called the Strand. Across the pavement, a lifeguard station jutted out of the sand, illuminated by a spotlight. Beyond it, she could hear the ocean rushing the beach in the darkness.

"Let's go upstairs," Sara said softly when they'd let themselves in the back door. "We'll get better reception up there."

Angel had no idea how Nico had gotten the key. Like so much about him and the power he wielded, it remained a mystery. She followed Sara up the stairs to a large living area with big windows. Sara set the bag with the laptop on the floor, then reached into one of her pockets for a headset. When both were in place, she handed a headset to Angel.

"It doesn't have a mic," Sara said, "so they won't be able to hear you. But at least you can listen."

Angel knew why it had been set up that way; they didn't need her voice in their ear. She tried not to feel stung. She was an observer, and she didn't have anything to contribute to this kind of mission. She was grateful Nico had relented to include her at all. She attached the headset to her ear and watched while Sara walked to the window and scanned the surrounding areas.

"In place," she said softly into the headset.

Nico's voice came through the headset. "Copy. Watch for my signal."

Sara pointed to the houses north of the one they were in. "Watch over there."

Angel did, and a moment later a faint blue light flashed near a yellow house two addresses up from where she and Sara would be monitoring the operation. Angel reached into her pocket, felt the weight of the gun. David was right there, only two houses away. Nico would get him out, and if Nico didn't, Angel would do it herself, whatever it took.

"Ten minutes," Nico's voice said in the headset.

"Let's set up," Sara said, bending to the duffel bag.

She removed the laptop and several power cords. Angel plugged them in while Sara pulled up the body cams. Then Angel could see the men, their faces still and tense. They must have had their mics off, because she could see their lips moving but couldn't hear what they were saying. A few seconds later, Mattia and Aldo disappeared from view, followed by Marco and Elia.

Sara tapped some keys on the laptop, then lined up six mini screens side by side. Angel watched as each pair of men moved into some kind of prearranged position. Her heart was hammering in her chest, her breath coming too fast, too shallow. She stood and walked to the window, wrapping her arms around her body, trying to keep from shaking.

She'd been so focused on David, that she'd forgotten something else; Nico would be in there, too. The two people who mattered most to her in the world at risk in the same situation. If Nico saved David, it probably meant they had both made it out alive. If he didn't, they could be lost to her forever. She almost doubled over from the fear and pain conjured by the thought.

"You don't have to watch," Sara said quietly behind her. "No one would blame you. You can stay right there. I'll keep you posted."

It was tempting, but that was the coward's way. David was in there, had lost two of his fingers and suffered god knew what else. And Nico was risking his life for her brother. For her. She would watch, would go to David the minute he was clear of the building. Would hold Nico close while she still could.

"It's okay," she said, returning to the carpet next to Sara. "I'm good."

"You sure?"

Angel nodded.

Sara reached out and squeezed her hand. "It will be okay."

"Two minutes," Nico's voice said over in her ear.

She and Sara turned their attention to the screen in front of them.

44

Nico stood next to Luca, both of them with their backs against the side of the house as they prepared to go in through the back. Somewhere at the front of the building, Marco and Elia were preparing to break in through the front door. Aldo and Mattia would climb in through the second floor balcony. Beach houses didn't have basements, and most of the attics in Southern California were unusable. Nico was betting that David was in one of the rooms on the second floor.

Normally Nico would be leading the charge from the front where it was most dangerous. But he'd made a promise to Angel that he would get her brother out alive, and he intended to see it done.

Personally.

But he would also kill Dante. That was personal, too, and he'd instructed the other men to do whatever they had to do to keep Dante alive until he could get there. They could shoot him to within an inch of his life for all Nico cared, but he would deliver the kill shot, and he would wait with him until the fucker's heart stopped beating. It was no less than the bastard deserved for what he'd done to Angel and her brother, and it was the only way Nico could be sure she would never have to worry about Dante again.

He checked his watch, then spoke into his headset. "Two minutes."

"Copy." Marco's voice came first. The others followed.

Nico took a deep breath, cleared his mind of everything, even Angel. He couldn't let himself think about her now. Not if he wanted to help her. She was the one thing that could undo him.

He watched the second hand tick on his watch. When it hit twelve for the second time, he spoke into the headset.

"Go time."

Luca bent his head to the lock on the door of the garage and went to work with a pick. It was open in less than twenty seconds. He waved Nico in.

The garage held a red Corvette and a black Escalade. A small set of stairs led to the house. Nico moved toward them with Luca on his heels. Sometimes these kinds of missions were grab and go — bust down doors, go in shooting, make a lot of noise to disorient everyone inside.

This was different. This was about getting a hostage out alive. And not just any hostage; the brother of the woman he loved. It pissed him off to be careful when he wanted to tear Dante's safe house apart, scare the living shit out of him, pull him and everyone in the house out of bed, kill them all while they were just awake enough to know he was the one pulling the trigger. But he would do it for her.

Angel...

He shook her name from his head and opened the door to the house.

45

Nico must have turned his mic back on, because she heard him tell the men it was time to go. She watched the screen that was projecting his body cam.

A darkened garage. Two cars in the shadows. A staircase leading to the house.

Then they were in, a long hallway stretched out in front of them. It was eerie watching them move down the unlit hall, their even breathing the only sound coming through the headsets. She couldn't tell if they were at the front of the house or the back, and she watched as they entered a massive gourmet kitchen, cleared it, then moved past it.

They had entered another hallway with several closed doors when Marco and Elia came into view from the opposite direction. She watched as they seemed to return hand signals that Nico must have been making behind his own body cam. A few seconds later, Nico moved past them, and Angel caught a glimpse of Mattia standing back from one of the doors in a position that made it clear he intended to kick down the door. He didn't though — not then anyway — and she watched as Nico headed for a set of stairs.

46

Nico turned to Luca, gesturing up the stairs. Marco And Elia had the downstairs doors covered, but unless they were forced to act, they would wait to go in until Nico gave them word that he had David. If everything was going according to plan, Aldo and Mattia were already on the second floor balcony, maybe even inside one of the upstairs bedrooms. They wouldn't speak into the headsets now unless they had to, just in case they were overheard.

He and Luca reached the top of the stairs and started down a wide main hallway. He was glad Luca didn't try to go first. As Underboss, it was protocol for Luca to protect him, but he had to know that Nico wouldn't have any of it. Not this time.

He started with the first closed door, quietly testing the knob to see if it was locked. It wasn't, and he continued to the next one without opening the door. He didn't think the second door would be David's prison either; if their recon was correct, it was the room attached to the balcony. He couldn't see Dante locking David up, then giving him an ocean view and a way to escape.

He tried it anyway, careful not to make any noise, and was unsurprised when the knob turned easily. He left the door closed and moved farther down the hall.

They passed a bathroom and came to another closed door. Also unlocked. He felt the first twinge of doubt.

What if they were wrong? What if David wasn't here at all?

He pushed the thought away. David was here. He could feel it.

There was one more door at the back of the house. He stood to the side, placed his hand on the knob, and turned.

Locked.

Nico looked at Luca and gestured from himself to the door, then pointed Luca to the first unlocked door. Luca would clear that room, Aldo and Mattia would take the second room on his command, entering through the balcony, and Nico would order one of them to the third room as soon as he could use his headset.

He stood back from the door and spoke into the mic.

"On my count; three, two, one…"

47

Angel's stomach tightened, her chest constricting as Nico's voice sounded in her ear. She glanced at Sara, staring at the screen with all the fear and intensity Angel felt, and wondered if Sara was as worried about Luca as Angel was about Nico.

She turned back to the computer as Nico counted down, and then the screen was a blur of movement as all hell broke loose, her headset filled with crashing and shouting.

* * *

Nico kicked in the door and simultaneously spoke into the headset. "One of you clear that third upstairs room."

He burst into a small bedroom with two boarded up windows, a mattress, and an attached bath. It took his eyes a moment to adjust to the room, but as soon as they did, he spotted a figure hunched in the corner.

"Show me your hands!" he shouted.

He couldn't afford to assume it was David, and he was relieved when the figure lifted his arms into the air.

"Don't shoot!"

Nico looked around, checking the attached bathroom to make sure it was clear before hurrying to David. The house had erupted into noise around them. Somewhere on the first floor, he heard the muffled sound of one of the silenced guns being fired. He was betting the shot came from Elia or Marco. Dante was too much of a narcissist to use silencers.

"I'm Nico Vitale," he said as he reached David. "I'm going to get you out of here." He helped David to his feet, surprised by how light he was. "Come with me and do as I say."

David wobbled a little on his feet, and Nico put David's arm around his neck and headed for the door. He tried not to think about the blood-soaked bandage on David's left hand. Nico had hoped Dante had been bluffing.

"Where's my sister?" David croaked as they headed for the door.

"She's safe," Nico said. "We have to focus on getting out of here."

He pushed David against the wall by the door, listening as glass shattered from one of the other rooms on the floor. He checked the hall to make sure it was clear, then grabbed David's arm and moved out.

* * *

Angel almost wept when David came into view. And then his voice was audible through Nico's headset. He was alive, well enough to speak, and only a few houses down. She watched as Nico helped him to the door. The hall came into view on Nico's body cam, and Angel could hear other sounds coming from elsewhere in the house; glass shattering, a series of muffled pops, shouting.

Then Nico and David were moving out into the hallway.

* * *

Nico wished like hell there was another exit at the back of the hall, but the only way to get David out of the house was to move past the three rooms currently under assault. He shoved David to his other side, trying to block Angel's brother with his body, and moved toward the staircase with his gun drawn.

"Where's Dante?" He asked David as they hurried down the hall.

"I... I don't know," David said.

Nico slowed as they approached the third door. Grunting sounds came from inside the room, and when Nico looked, he saw Aldo pummeling a man he didn't recognize with the butt of his weapon.

He continued down the hall, slowing when they neared the second door. Gunfire exploded through the house. Nico looked at David and was momentarily torn. He needed to keep his men safe, but getting David out was their number one priority. He dared a look in the room as he hustled David past it and was relieved to see that Mattia had disarmed the man inside. They were going at it hand to hand. Nothing Nico could do to help without leaving David's side. And that he would not do.

He continued to the staircase.

* * *

Angel held her breath as Nico looked into each of the rooms. She couldn't see the faces of the men fighting, couldn't tell who was winning, but Nico kept his arm around David's waist as he eased David down the hall. Just like he promised.

She wondered how many men were in the house. Were Nico and Luca and the others outmatched? The gun was heavy in her jacket pocket.

* * *

Luca was inside the first room, unleashing his rage on Vincent.

The traitor.

Vincent was bigger than Luca, but Luca was strong and fast. They circled each other, Vincent with a wicked looking knife pointed at Luca.

Luca's hands were empty, and Nico itched to help by unleashing a few rounds on the bastard who had betrayed them. He moved past the room instead, hustling David down the stairs as a voice shouted in his headset.

"Elia is down," Marco said. "I repeat, Elia is down. And Santoro is getting away through the back door."

"Go get him," Nico shouted as he reached the first floor.

"Can't, boss," Marco huffed, out of breath. A split second later, Nico heard a wet thwack. "Still got two men down here, and I'm not leaving Elia."

He heard the sound of wood splintering and continued into the first floor hall, then hurried for the back door with David still at his side.

* * *

Angel dug her fingernails into her palm as Marco's voice came through the headset. What did down mean? Dead? Or just injured?

She watched Nico head down the hall and burst through a door. A narrow alley came into view, lined with houses. For a second everything seemed to spin, and she couldn't make sense of anything broadcast via the body cam as Nico looked right, then left.

And then, about two houses away in the alley, she saw the figure running.

Dante.

* * *

"Freeze, motherfucker," Nico said, shoving David against the garage door and pointing his weapon at the retreating figure.

Dante glanced back, stumbled a little, raised his weapon. Nico lined him up in his sights and was about to fire when he felt the hit to his shoulder from behind. It was like a ball of fire tunneling through skin, tendon, muscle. It went quickly numb, and Nico steadied his arm, determined to finish the job he'd come to do.

He squeezed off one shot just as another arrow of fire shot into his back. And this time he went down, the sky tilting above him as he hit the pavement.

* * *

Angel stood, her heart squeezing as Nico fell. He turned his head, and she got a picture of Dante crawling toward him. He turned his head the other way, and she saw David, huddled against the house.

But that wasn't all. Another man was there, too. And he was coming toward Nico with his gun drawn.

She was out the door before she was even aware of making the decision.

"Angel!" Sara's voice sounded behind her as she hurried down the stairs of the empty house. "Angel, don't!"

* * *

Nico reached for his gun. It was close. So close. He could see Dante inching toward him. He didn't know how serious his own injuries were, but whatever happened, Dante wasn't leaving this alley alive.

He dared a glance in the other direction and saw a big man he didn't recognize coming toward him, one of Locke's weapons, complete with silencer, in his hands. Nico wondered where he'd gotten it, if any of his men were beyond saving.

But that wasn't his problem now. Kill Dante. Make sure David made it back to Angel.

Those were his tasks.

He stretched a little farther, his fingers brushing against his gun laying in the shadow of the house. Dante was looking at him with single-minded determination, raising his weapon just as Nico closed his fingers around his own. He got the gun into position in his hand before lifting it into the air, then aimed and fired in almost the same motion.

A flash of light burst from Dante's gun at the same time. Nico felt the hit to his chest as he watched the hole open up in Dante's forehead. He collapsed onto the pavement like a wet rag.

* * *

Angel turned the corner of the alley just as Dante fired. She saw the bullet hit Nico, saw his body jerk against the pavement.

"No!" Was that her voice? She couldn't be sure.

And then she was rushing toward him, the gun somehow in her hand, pointed at the one remaining man who stood between her and Nico.

She was almost there when he spun to face her. She hardly had time to aim before she fired, sloppy and not at all like Nico had showed her. Time seemed to slow down as the man's bullet made its way toward her body, her finger squeezing the trigger of the gun in her hand over and over again. She was barely aware of the man's own weapon firing, barely aware of the bullet entering her stomach as the man fell to the ground. Then she was on the ground, Nico only inches away, his face turned toward hers, eyes closed.

"Ange!" She looked up into David's face. "Ange... Oh, my god... You've been shot."

"I'm fine." She tried to smile. "You'll be fine, too."

He lifted her head into his lap and started screaming. "Help! Help me!"

Angel turned her head, watched as Nico's eyes flickered open. He moved his hand, reached for her. She felt his fingers close around hers as the world went black.

48

She parked along the curb and got out of the car, careful not to pull her stitches. The cemetery was illuminated by a half-moon, and she had a sudden flash of that last moonless night on the beach. She remembered it like it was yesterday: Nico's hand in hers, his lips brushing her skin like a whisper, the last time she'd felt like everything might be okay.

A week and a lifetime ago.

She walked up a small hill to the marker, still surrounded by flowers from the service earlier that day. She'd been there, of course. Had attended the mass and then continued onto the gravesite with everyone else, watched as black suited men spoke in low tones about the massacre in Los Angeles, about the fate of the Vitale family, the Syndicate.

But she hadn't looked at the casket. It made everything too real to think of Nico, her Nico, there. She still wasn't ready to imagine him gone, but she needed to be with him, needed to tell him the things she hadn't said when he was alive. She would have liked to go to Maine, to walk their beach and look at the lighthouse. But there was too much to be done.

She touched her hand to one of the scarlet roses propped up next to the marker, rubbed the silken petals between her fingers, then lowered herself to the grass. She looked at the words etched into the granite.

Nico Anthony Vitale
Son, Friend, Warrior
November 20, 1986 - April 16, 2015

She wished there was a word that encompassed everything he'd been to her; lover, challenger, protector. It was true that he'd been the instrument of her lost innocence, but that would have happened anyway. She was glad it had happened with him. That he'd been there to help her find the way, to teach her that she was stronger than she ever imagined.

Now, finally, she knew who she was.

She plucked the grass around her legs, remembering that last night. Would anything have been different if she'd stayed in the house with Sara? She shook her head. She knew it wouldn't. She'd been over it a hundred times. Nico only would have died sooner, and she wouldn't have been able to look into his eyes one last time. She was glad she'd been able to do that. She'd felt his love in that moment, and she had to believe he had felt hers. Believing that made everything worthwhile — the emergency surgery to remove the bullet in her belly, the stitches that would leave scars, David's PTSD, the hole in her heart.

She would gladly do it all again if it meant Nico had felt her love in the end.

She would live. David would live. Luca was wrecked, but he would live, too.

It was only Nico who was gone. Or the only one gone that they would miss.

She leaned her forehead against the granite marker, let it cool her skin as hot tears leaked from her eyes.

"I love you, Nico," she whispered. "I've loved you since the beginning, will love you forever. You were better than all of us."

She could still feel him. Could still smell him. Could still conjure his touch, his kiss, the way he looked at her. It hurt so much to remember. She felt like the pain of it would stop her heart cold. But it hurt worse to think there might come a day when she would forget. When Nico's image would be nothing but a faded memory.

People will tell you who they are if you listen.

Nico had told her who he was from the beginning. She just hadn't been listening close enough. He'd been a man who loved her with his whole heart. Who would compromise everything he worked for, everything he believed in, for her.

A man who would die for her.

She swiped at her tears, touched her fingertips to her lips and pressed them against the valley of his name, fought the sobs shaking her body. He'd told her who he was. Had shown her.

Now it was time for her to show him.

49

Her heels clicked on the marble floor of the Prudential building as they made their way past the guard desk to the elevator; Luca in front of her, Elia and Marco on either side.

They got into the elevator. Luca pressed the button for the forty-eighth floor, and they rose upward in silence. She surveyed her reflection in the mirror without emotion. It should have been strange to see herself in the slim gray skirt, the blood red jacket over the white blouse, the heels that gave her an extra four inches. Her hair was pulled back into a neat chignon, her makeup understated but polished enough to make her look a couple years older than her twenty-five years. But it was her eyes that had changed the most. They were still green, only now there was something hard and flinty in them, and she remembered Nico's animal eyes, the danger she'd seen lurking there the first time she'd seem him.

The elevator slowed to a stop. She caught sight of the gun holstered under Luca's suit jacket as he maneuvered in front of her and knew Marco and Elia were similarly armed. It reassured her, but not because she was scared for herself. They had made her unbreakable. Nothing they could take from her would hurt as much as losing Nico.

Now she could survive anything.

The elevator doors slid open, and Luca led the way into the lobby of Rossi Development. The receptionist stood, her mouth open in alarm as they bypassed her desk. Then they were walking down the long hallway Angel remembered from the last time she'd been there.

She opened the double doors to her father's office as Luca, Elia, and Marco continued next door to the office occupied by Frank. She could hear Frank's protests as she made her way around her father's desk. She couldn't tell what he was saying, but he was obviously agitated, and a moment later she heard the wet thwack of a hard punch. A few seconds later, Elia and Marco dragged Frank past the open door of her father's office.

Her office now.

She stood at the desk, ran her hands along the leather blotter. Frank was just the beginning. The men had a long list of people who would experience similar exits — both from the legal and illegal arms of the Rossi businesses. The three men would stay with her in Boston until they'd cleaned house. Angel would work until every one of the people responsible for Nico's death, every single person who had turned on him, paid with their lives.

Then she would burn the whole operation to the ground. New York, too. Nico deserved a better legacy. She would give it to him.

She sat at the chair behind her father's desk, took a deep breath.

How far would you go to protect the ones you love?

Not too long ago, she hadn't known the answer. Now there was another part to the question; how far would you go to avenge the ones you love? As she leaned forward in her father's chair and reached for the phone, she finally knew the answer.

As far as it took.

ORDER LAWLESS, THE FINAL BOOK IN THE MOB BOSS TRILOGY, NOW

Reviews are such a big help to authors and readers! Please let others know how you enjoyed this book by leaving a review.

Please find me online. I'd love to get to know you!

Website

Facebook

Twitter

Instagram

Continue to Lawless Sneak Peek…

Lawless

1

Angel Rossi opened her eyes all at once, fighting disorientation in the moment before she remembered where she was; the sofa in her office —formerly her father's office.

It wasn't unusual for her to sleep a couple of hours on the sofa and then work until morning when she would run home for a shower and change of clothes. In the four months since she'd taken over her father's businesses — and the Syndicate's Boston territory — she'd spent almost every waking hour at Rossi Development.

She stretched on the sofa and checked her phone. Two am, which meant she'd been dozing for almost three hours. She would need to work through the night to finish auditing the financials on the offshore company that looked to be an off-the-books payroll service for the crooked cops who worked for her father.

She wondered if Luca was still in the office next door. He'd been her almost constant companion since Nico's death, but she knew he missed Sara in New York, even if he thought he was being slick about keeping his feelings for her under the radar. Angel would have to send him back soon. Allow him to run New York properly, the way Nico had intended when he'd appointed Luca Underboss before his death.

Nico...

She shouldn't have worried that she would forget him. She could see his face as clearly as if she'd seen him yesterday, could still feel his hands on her naked body, his breath against her hair when he pulled her close in the middle of the night. He was as real as ever, and sometimes the permanence of his absence hit her out of the blue, the worst kind of surprise. She would double over then, heaving, gasping for air, sure the blood was turning to sludge in her veins, that her heart was slowly coming to a stop without him.

She was always surprised when she woke up, still breathing, the next morning. She forced herself to put one foot in front of the other even when it seemed impossible. It was what Nico would want, and she focused with obsessive single-mindedness on remaking her father's empire — and plotting revenge against the people who had supported Dante in his bid to oust Nico.

Raneiro had come to visit shortly after she'd removed Frank Morra. The head of the Syndicate had been impassive as he'd quizzed her about her plans for the Boston territory. She wasn't fooled. Possession was nine-tenths of the law, but she knew he had concerns. Her father hadn't intended for her to take over when he died, hadn't even bothered to tell Angel about his business with the Syndicate. She knew what Raneiro was thinking.

What does this girl think she's doing? She's in way over her head.

It might have been true in the beginning, when she'd been driven more by fury than ambition. But her anger had fueled a sustained determination to dismantle the machine that had taken Nico from her and ruined her chances of having a normal life. That had traumatized David to the point that he could hardly leave the brownstone even now, months after Dante kidnapped him and cut off two of his fingers in an effort to gain control of the New York territory.

Dante had been the instrument, but he hadn't been alone. Men had defected from every family in the months before Nico's death. All of them had worked with Dante in one capacity of another. Offered him help, support, resources. She had made it her mission to destroy every one of them.

She was learning the books at Rossi development inside and out. Learning where the money was hidden, how it was laundered. Learning which cops were on the payroll, which men had aided her father in the murder of Nico's parents. And now she knew who was involved in the most despicable of the Syndicate's income streams — child pornography, human trafficking, bad loans to people who were already down on their luck, identity theft of innocent people.

She was slowly picking at the threads that would unravel everything.

She sat up as something rustled nearby. Was it outside the office? The janitors usually didn't come until later, and everyone else was gone except Luca. He rarely left her alone, and when he did go back to the apartment he was renting downtown, he made sure Marco or Elia had eyes on her. It had been disconcerting at first, but she'd gotten used to it. After what happened in Los Angeles, she didn't trust anyone, and she needed to stay alive long enough to finish the job she'd started and make sure David was back on his feet.

She heard the sound again, then saw something shift out of the corner of her eye. She stood, heart pounding, and reached for the gun she'd set on the coffee table before she'd gone to sleep. She'd rejected David's suggestion that she might have PTSD, too. That she could benefit from counseling. She'd gone to the shooting range instead, hired an instructor, practiced until she had a ninety percent kill ratio at seventy-five feet.

She scanned the office, her eyes coming to rest on a shadowy figure leaning against the wall across from her.

She raised the gun, thumbed off the safety. "I suggest you identify yourself," she said. "Unless you'd like your DNA to do it for you."

The figure stepped forward, arms raised in surrender, hands empty. But that was all easy to register, easier than the face that slowly came into view in the faint light spilling from the lamp on the desk.

She shook her head. "It… It can't be."

He stepped closer, and she was assaulted by the smell of him, the scent of leather and soap and something else now. Pine?

He gently took the gun from her hand and set it back on the coffee table. Then he met her gaze, and she knew it was true. His face was thinner, but it was him, the amber eyes piercing hers in the darkness, the set of his shoulders as uncompromising as ever under his white T-shirt and a familiar leather jacket.

He touched his knuckles to her face, ran them gently down her cheek, his eyes locked on hers. She couldn't breathe, didn't dare move. She registered with detachment that her face was wet, tears streaming from her eyes.

"I'm sorry, Angel," he said.

She lifted a hand and cracked it hard across his face.

Acknowledgments

Since beginning this journey with Ruthless, I've been fortunate enough to meet countless people who have supported me in ways big and small.

Special thanks go to friend, mentor, and author M.J. Rose, who continues to light the way by supporting and encouraging countless writers with her own special brand of kindness and innovation. I don't know where I would be without her, and without AuthorBuzz, who gave Ruthless the push it needed to land in the hands of so many readers its first month.

Much gratitude to all the romance writers in the Indie community who have gone before me and have shared information on covers, formatting, readership, and marketing. I'm not sure I've ever met a more generous group of people. It feels in many ways like coming home.

Thanks to Caitlin Greer for her beautiful formatting, and to Laura Benson for line editing, both of which had to occur on a very tight deadline. You guys have the patience of saints!

Thanks also to Isabel Robello for my gorgeous covers (and for also being patient when I change my mind — I'm sensing a theme here). Can't wait to get started on covers for the next series!

Thank you to Kenneth, Rebekah, Andrew, and Caroline, who graciously gave up a lot of summer fun so I could get the Mob Boss books out on time, and who cheerfully listen to me talk about characters, plot summaries, deadlines, and marketing. It's pretty awesome when your kids care enough to ask, "How's the book doing, Mom?"

And of course, my biggest thanks of all go to you, dear reader, for taking a chance on my books, rooting for Nico and Angel, spreading the word, reviewing online, and warming my heart with your enthusiasm and support. I mean this in the most literal sense possible…

I couldn't do it without you.